Counterpo

Counterpoint

ANNA ENQUIST

TRANSLATED FROM THE DUTCH BY
JEANNETTE K. RINGOLD

UWAP
UWA PUBLISHING

First published in 2010 by
UWA Publishing
Crawley, Western Australia 6009
www.uwap.uwa.edu.au

UWAP is an imprint of UWA Publishing
a division of The University of Western Australia

THE UNIVERSITY OF
WESTERN AUSTRALIA
Achieving International Excellence

Publication has been made possible with the financial support from the
Foundation for the Production and Translation of Dutch Literature.

This book is copyright. Apart from any fair dealing for the purpose of private
study, research, criticism or review, as permitted under the *Copyright Act
1968*, no part may be reproduced by any process without written permission.
Enquiries should be made to the publisher.

Copyright © 2008 ANNA ENQUIST/DE ARBEIDERSPERS
Translation Copyright © 2010 JEANNETTE K. RINGOLD

The moral right of the author has been asserted.

A full CIP record for this book is available from
the National Library of Australia.

Cover photograph: Getty Images

Typeset in 12pt Bembo by Lasertype
Printed by McPherson's Printing Group

Aria

The woman with the pencil leaned over the table and read a pocket score of the Goldberg Variations. The pencil was made of a special black wood. It had a heavy silver cap that concealed a pencil sharpener. The pencil was poised above an empty notebook. Next to the score lay cigarettes and a lighter. A small metal ashtray, a shiny and compact present from a friend, was on the table.

The woman was simply called "woman," perhaps "mother." There were naming problems. There were many problems. In the woman's consciousness, memory problems lay at the surface. The aria that she was looking at, the theme on which Bach composed his Goldberg Variations, reminded her of those times when she had studied this music. When the children were small. Before. After. She was not searching for those memories. A child on each thigh and then, with her arms around the children's bodies, strive to play that theme; enter the Recital Hall of the Concertgebouw; watch the pianist walk onto the stage, wait breathlessly for the unadorned octave of the first note—feel the daughter's elbow: 'Mummy, that's *our* song!' There was no need for that now. She wanted to think only of the daughter. The daughter as a baby, as a girl, as a young woman.

The memories withered into grey clichés that would not interest anyone. She would not be able to recount anything about the daughter; she didn't know the daughter. Write about that, she thought angrily. Even a flanking movement is a movement; a negative also shows an image. But she still didn't know whether silence is also sound.

Before she sat down at the table, she read an article about the concept of time in a South American Indian tribe. The people of that tribe see the past ahead of them and feel the future at their backs. Their faces are turned toward the past, and what is still to come will come as an unforeseen attack. This way of experiencing time, according to the author of the article, can still be found in language and in grammatical constructions. This remarkable, reverse perspective was discovered by a linguist.

The woman realised that she had once read this same account with the ancient Greeks as the main characters. Despite years of instruction in Greek language and literature, she had never noticed it. Perhaps she had still been too young then. Too much future, inconceivable not to keep your eyes focused on it.

The woman was not yet what you would call an old woman, but she certainly was well on her way. She had an extensive past.

The past. That which has passed. Imagine that you, as an Indian, looked at it as a matter of course, that you woke up with it, dragged it around all day long, that it presented itself as the landscape of dreams. Not so strange, thought the woman, actually that's how it was. She closed her eyes and imagined the future in the figure of a man who was standing behind her, whom she didn't see.

The future had wrapped his sturdy arms around her, perhaps even rested his chin on her hair. He held her tight. The future was taller than she. Did she lean back against his chest? Did she feel his warm belly? She knew that he looked over her shoulder with her at her past. Surprised, interested, indifferent?

With enormous concern, that's what she assumed, always trusting. After all, he was her personal future. She breathed against his right arm that lay high against her chest. Actually, around her neck. If he eased that arm slightly, she would be able to get more air and speak.

The future pulled her against him, so forcefully that she had to take a small step backward, and another. She resisted. The past had to remain near, in full view. The pressure of his arm became unpleasant; it seemed as though the future wanted to drag her along forcibly, compelling her to step backward steadily, with small, almost elegant dance steps. She dug her heels in. The embrace became suffocating; she choked in the arms of the future. His name is Time. He will lead her away from what she loves; he will take her to places where she does not want to be.

The percussionists in the conservatory were a different kind of student. They carried on in a partially rebuilt church, rolled their own cigarettes, and started late. When they joined orchestra class, they didn't mix with the string players. They moved like construction workers at the back of the stage, setting up xylophones, hanging bells from scaffolds, tuning kettledrums the size of washtubs. They wore sneakers and yelled unintelligibly to one another.

Of all of us they are the most talented in organising time, thought the woman, then still young, sitting at the back of the hall and looking at the orchestra getting ready. The percussionists don't fuss about time; they don't turn it into a philosophical problem. They hear the beat; they create the rhythms above it; they translate what they feel into movement. They are engaged in waiting and striking, waiting and striking, striking. The ability to hear patterns in a series of exactly the same beeps is innate. We can't do otherwise. Organising is a characteristic of our brain, of us, one of our traits, a survival strategy, a sickness. This is our way of making the chaotic, muddy soup around us into a recognisable and reassuring setting. We have forgotten that nothing makes sense at all, that we ourselves provide the distinctness and the trust. Someone should research the connection between organising patterns and character traits. Why does one person hear 4/4 time and another, 6/8?

Why did she have to think of all this—it was neither here nor there.

It was about Time tugging at her neck like an impatient lover, forcing her to walk backward, step by step, so that her view of what was past became less and less distinct.

With a great leap back in time, thought the woman. Or furtively, in a dark grey disguise, crawl back to an afternoon filled with songs, filled with music, a child at my right and a child at my left. Then see that scene as intensely as when it took place. Feeling, smelling, and hearing the same as then.

It doesn't work like that; you never feel the same. Of course you can look back ("look ahead"), but the time that has meanwhile elapsed, what has happened in that time span, colours your perception. A thing can never be the same during two moments in time; at any rate it can't be perceived as "the same" because the observer has changed.

Just look at the Goldberg Variations. You play the aria. Oh no, thought the woman, I'll never play that aria again. Fine, you played the aria, past tense, that quiet, tragic song. It's a sarabande, just listen, a stately tempo and accent on the second beat of every bar, a slow, perhaps static, dance. You played the aria with dedication, with passion, with the commitment to do it perfectly. Toward the end, the long notes became garlands of sixteenths, but the serious cadence was not lost. You didn't give in to the temptation to play more softly, in a whisper at the end, and to conclude with a barely audible sigh. No, even then you let those melancholy garlands of notes swell above the calmly ambling bass line, not hurrying, preferably slowing down unnoticeably—nice and loud, with force. Until the end.

After the aria, Bach composed thirty variations in which he held to the harmonic scheme and the chord sequence of the sarabande. That bass line was the constant against which he created original variations. Finally the aria was played again. The same sarabande, not one note more or less. But was it the same? Yes, those were the same notes. No, the player and the listener could not erase the thirty Variations between the first and the last appearance of the sarabande. Even though it was identical to the first one, you heard the second aria differently because something had happened in the meantime. You couldn't go back to the time when you had not yet heard the Variations.

Oh, she was so eager to study the Goldberg Variations; she was caught in the aria as in a net. 'Don't start on it,' said the teacher, 'such a fuss with those hands crossing, a lot of work and little to show for it. Take a nice partita, a pleasant toccata, the Chromatic Fantasy! The woman agreed readily; the advice was correct and reasonable. But right after her final examination she had placed the score on her music rack.

When there is no performance or time pressure, all depends on discipline that you can feed only with passion. She worked out the music, as much as she was able to at the time. What do you have going for you after conservatory training? Virtuosity, control, too much of an ear for the impressive, for outward show. For these Variations a new humility is needed, except that you can never play them from a position of humility. The technique demands superiority.

Technique means dexterity, muscular strength, automatic movements, agility. It is easy to fill hours training in these matters. You feel your muscles, and that is satisfying. The body tells you that you have spent your time well and usefully. Doesn't it say "Klavierübung," keyboard practice, on the title page of the Goldberg Variations? That's what it is. Your physical technique is at its peak around the final examination. You'll never again be in such form.

It is misleading. Technique is not only control of muscle movement but also control of thought. You *have* to think: listen to the leading voice; anticipate placing hands and fingers; think ahead to give shape to tempo, dynamic and phrasing. A great part of the training takes place in your head. This demands even more discipline than studying at the keyboard. Sitting at the piano, the slowness of the body ensures that you don't get up, but thoughts are so light, so unexpectedly nimble, that it's almost impossible to keep them in line.

She was a slave to her playing body during her first study of the Variations. That's why nothing came of it, at least no more than an exercise in dexterity. She studied from the Peters Edition and played the notes as they were presented to her. During her training she had been able to transform the most peculiar and most complicated scores into movement and ultimately, into sound; hence the strange situations on the keyboard, the ones that arose because Bach created his Variations for an instrument with two manuals, should not be that problematic. Yet there were problems. Which hand high on the key, the hand that had the melody or the hand that played the second part? Besides, which was the melody and which the counterpoint? In polyphony all voices have equal value. The fingerings in the score were useless to her, since they had been made by an old harpsichordist with preconceptions and idiosyncrasies. She thought. She could see him in front of her, the imaginary harpsichord virtuoso. A paunch under a tightly buttoned cardigan, long hair carefully pasted across his bald head. A disapproving look on his fleshy face. Actually, it was lucky her fingers fitted between the black keys so that she could play high on the key with one hand, while the other one played lower on the same key. There were pianists who removed the open lid behind the keyboard when performing the Goldberg Variations. Then you looked directly into the unpainted interior of the instrument, then you saw the hammers fly up, strike the strings and come down. Because the eye registered this with a fractional delay, you were looking into the past; what you saw had just happened.

She finished the Variations in several months. In this case "finished" meant that she could play everything from the page. From this specific score where she herself had put in fingerings and sketched in hand positions. Another edition had immediately caused her to flounder and miss, had confused and disoriented her. A weakness. Did she really know the Goldberg Variations, or did she know its reflection in this image of notes—what was real, what was a copy, a replica? The question was how solidly the Variations were anchored in her thinking, in her head, in her cerebral cortex. At the spinal cord level everything went like clockwork—one look at the paper set in motion the imprinted movements of her arms, wrists and fingers. But sometimes the Variation that appeared when the page was turned was a surprise. She didn't think carefully. Without the music, she could probably not name the Variations in the right order. Certainly, the beginning, the ending as well, and the last five or so. In between them it was a muddle, exactly as predicted by educational psychology. Was it because of the stage of her life? The children were small and captivating. At any moment she had to be able to jump from the piano bench to get something to drink, to read to them, to answer a question. The times when they slept were just long enough to study one difficult passage; there was never enough time to play everything through, to adjust tempi, to be able to discover larger units. Yes, blame the children. She hadn't made enough effort; she had let herself be led by the notes and had lost herself in them.

She didn't know much about Bach at the time, even though she had played tremendously difficult pieces by him, and not just a few. Early Bach, late Bach. Köthen, Leipzig, first wife, second wife? No idea. What interested her was how you could perform those fast little notes of Variation 17 non legato, softly and yet evenly. She had studied the left-hand arrangement that Brahms had made of the famous violin Chaconne, when she had been bothered for a while by her right hand, but the similarities between that piece and the Goldberg Variations had not struck her. She had been nice and busy with the leaps and the tremolos.

She had read somewhere that everything happens twice, the first time as a tragedy and the second time as a farce. She simply read too much. This remark was attributed to various sages. The woman at the table, the woman with the pencil, didn't care who had said it, only whether it was true. It was up to her to make the remark true, at least partly. Nothing stood in her way now, after thirty years, to practise the Goldberg Variations again. As a farce.

She hesitated. Slowly she leafed through the small pocket score. Groups of three, she thought, and each group consists of a "free" piece, a virtuoso piece and a canon. To her, those canons seemed the thread leading the player through the work. One voice literally imitates the other in the first canon, almost as if they were making fun of each other. Underneath the tug-of-war of these two voices hums a restless bass. She moved from one canon to the next. The two voices separate more and more; the second voice answers one tone higher, then in the third canon, at the third between them. The voices become increasingly separated. In some canons the answer is given in inversion, the whole melody is played upside-down. Further, further. Canon at the octave, the same notes, but separated by the perfect interval. At the ninth, for the first time without bass, only the voices that ornament each other with a poignant difference at the starting point. In the place where the last canon should be, the thirtieth Variation, she encountered the strange "quodlibet," a four-voice composition of song fragments. She snapped shut the score.

This time she wanted to see the whole. A farce is more difficult than a tragedy, say actors, who should know. She had to be thoroughly prepared if she was going to study this work again. You didn't prepare for a tragedy; it happened to you. But hadn't she been happy during that first period of study? What tragedy lurked in the image of a young mother with two children? Maybe the tragedy lay in the intensity of the experience. The feeling of exacting motherhood had completely absorbed her. She had disappeared into it; no, motherhood had disappeared into her; there had been nothing else beside it; that she used to play the Variations for her children had filled her to the tips of her fingers. Tragedy left no room for reflection and denied the distance needed to see the whole. Tragedy is a wave that drags you along, a stream of lava, a whirlwind. For a farce you take a seat in the observation post. You observe, you compare, you ensure accurate timing. That's how it should be this time.

Comparative textual research. That stupid Peters Edition—she couldn't cope with it. The annoying shifting of your hands over each other in order to satisfy the requirements of the notes on the page—she was no longer in the mood. It should be possible to change his voices around, to play with one hand what was noted down for the other hand. That became the first goal: to have a score that would be rather easy to play. No concessions, she wasn't here to imitate a harpsichord. Bach can always be played; he is universal and is performed on guitar, accordion, and on the grand piano as well.

In the music shop they didn't know what she was talking about. The man behind the counter produced a stack of Goldberg editions—an "Urtext" by Henle, the Peters, a Schirmer edition by Kirkpatrick. She took them home, even though Kirkpatrick was a harpsichordist, and probably dead. She remembered his Goldberg recording on two long-playing records. The sixties. Half of the thick book consisted of text, angry, accusing text. Why, the old harpsichordist shouted in despair, why does no one know that you ALWAYS start a pralltriller with the upper second? It was described in all the authoritative texts; he had said it himself for years, and yet people persisted in their errors. He also sounded serious warnings about the instrument. The pianist—in this context the term seemed a dirty word—had to realise that he was playing a TRANSCRIPTION. You should set aside pianistic expressive possibilities; they were inappropriate and would be a sign of bad taste. She was almost ashamed of her unwieldy, noisy and common grand piano.

Kirkpatrick also had an opinion about fingerings: in certain cases, thank God, the thumb was allowed on the black keys, but unfortunately he gave no practical examples.

In his edition there were no fingerings. Not one. The pianist had to find them himself, he wrote, because 'there is no better remedy for laziness than work.'

Hence, a totally masochistic purchase. The reason the book was in her bag anyway was because the alternative versions of the score had some fast variations printed in thin, grey ink. In those alternatives the fingerings had been shifted exactly as she wished. They were printed above the original lines so that you could easily follow the original part-writing. He, Kirkpatrick, had done it to make it possible to play at sight. As if anyone could ever sight-read these variations! It was a gift; it worked out extremely well. Copy, cut, throw away the original rules, and paste the alternatives on a blank piece of paper. Find fingerings. Work.

For the woman at the table, practising the piano was more a narcotic than anything else. She had to force herself to maintain her sense of the whole. If I've got everything down more or less, she thought, then I should start to practise the Variations in groups, for an overview. Ten groups of three, five of six, two of fifteen, and then…the whole. And read something, she thought, a musicological treatise about the work, a biography of the composer. Not Thomas Bernard's *The Loser* again, not all sorts of opinions and facts concerning Glenn Gould again—not the feelings evoked by the work, but the background of the work itself.

Who wrote it? The mature, adult Bach. The composer, the husband, the father. In Leipzig, where he supervised the wretchedly poor and undisciplined boys' choir. The woman had been in Bach's house opposite the Thomaskirche; she had sat and smoked in the courtyard; she had listened to harpsichord sounds that had vanished centuries ago.

For whom did he write it? For his first child, Wilhelm Friedemann, the oldest son from Bach's first marriage. His favorite, his virtuoso. The one who would be able to shine with the Variations in his new position in Dresden. Bach visited his son there in 1741. Did they share a room; did they talk in the dark; did they sing themes and song fragments to each other? Friedemann was around ten years old when his mother died; he might have spoken with his father about her before they fell asleep. Were there any reproaches? A year after the death of his wife, Bach remarried a twenty-one-year old soprano, Maria Magdalena. They set out for Leipzig with the entire household, and every year they had another child. What had Friedemann thought of that?

The woman at the table thought about the violin Chaconne. It is said that Bach composed it in memory of his first wife. How could he, stricken by such enormous grief, fall in love with the young singer? Did his grief disappear into the Chaconne? Was he free after that? At any rate he was in love and wrote simple, charming keyboard music for his new spouse who wanted to learn to play the harpsichord from the small music book that her husband put together for her. How touching. The man who had written the Brandenburg Concertos and had created the Well-Tempered Clavier wrote small minuets and gavottes for his young wife.

And the sarabande that would become the aria of the Goldberg Variations, the seed from which all thirty variations would grow, Anna Magdalena copied these notes into her little lesson book. Did she not hear the sorrow of this simple melody? Was she deaf to those last eight measures in which the composer fights off his despair, trying his utmost to keep his footing?

There must have been an unbridgeable difference between Bach and his second wife. She, at first losing herself in a life full of the most wonderful music, moving through the house between harpsichords, violas, overflowing music cupboards. He, determined to start anew, but wading through the sticky past, probably filled with gratitude—and with a grief that he couldn't share with anyone and only hinted at in the music he wrote. He knew the perverse unreliability of life, understood that nothing and no one offered protection against loss. You walked down familiar roads and suddenly an abyss opened in which everything disappeared, without a sound.

Perhaps he thought of that, lying next to his son in Dresden, listening to his breathing, staring into the dark with eyes wide open. Possibly his head was spinning; he could no longer recall the dimensions of the unfamiliar room; who knows if he was perhaps resting on the edge of an abyss and would fall into the silent void as soon as he turned? Sweating, Bach lay in his guest bed in the city of Dresden, without anything to hold onto and without a view of the whole.

The woman with the pencil imagined how Bach forced himself to think about the Variations. A beautifully bound, gold-embossed copy lay in his luggage, wrapped in a piece of linen. Tomorrow he would hand it to the Prince or the Elector or whatever the man who employed Friedemann wished to be called. For Friedemann himself he had brought a less elaborate copy. The Variations! In the ominous silence Bach reconstructed them anew. In his mind he played them in the correct tempo. He strung them one to the other; the voices spread out in his head, pushing aside despair and fear. He told himself a story without words and fell asleep before Variation 16.

The woman sighed longingly. She wasn't that far yet. The Variations like beads on a string, in the correct and logical order; clicking the two identical arias together as a conclusion—the beginning into the end. Or: the ending audible in the beginning.

Practice was the only way. Search for the moment when the work started to shrink, when the chaos of details, the overwhelming abundance, yielded to structure. For that you had to immerse yourself stubbornly in the smallest fragments. There was no other way. Not until everything, every note, was thought out at the most detailed level, overpowered, and had become part of the motor system. Only then could her attention climb one step higher and her perspective expand.

Patience. Persistence. Some day, at an unexpected moment, the vista would open up and the Variations would lie there in a configuration that was so obvious that you wouldn't understand how you could ever have been confused about it.

You could describe a life in this way, thought the woman. With her pencil she drew circles on the paper, connected by a line. This same harmony in ever-changing fans of forms and sounds, that in the end gave a complete picture of what had happened. Of the past that lay in front of her.

She had to get in. She had to dare, as when children, in nonchalant despair, jump off the high diving board for the first time. Jump in.

The television showed a programme about Glenn Gould. He recorded the Goldberg Variations twice, at the beginning and at the end of his career as a pianist. It was night. The woman sat in front of the screen with her legs crossed and looked at the bloated, unhealthy-looking pianist. He would die before very long. Death was already hidden under his skin, but now, but still, he bent intently over the keyboard. His thick glasses with the black frames almost touched the ivory keys. He sat on the edge of an old, wooden chair with a worn-out seat. During the first recording of the piece, in 1955, the chair was still intact. He had been a boy then, with a shock of curls and a checked shirt. Of course the record company had advised him to choose a more accessible piece for this—his first—record, something that the public would recognise and appreciate immediately, something that was easier to listen to. That had been out of the question; the tragedy was going to occur, and young Glenn Gould recorded the Goldberg Variations in the Columbia studio in New York.

While listening to the recorded fragments, he danced with closed eyes through the room, singing, conducting, accompanying the melody line with grand gestures. The woman had seen photos of this. Innocence, naïveté, complete seriousness. You could shrug your shoulders; you could scream with laughter; you could shake your head pityingly at someone who took himself so seriously. But you didn't, for what you saw was youth itself, the tragedy of being young. Respectful silence was the proper response.

The film she was looking at dated from twenty-seven years ago. Twenty-seven years. A whole life, definitely too short, which the pianist had obviously exhausted completely. Sometimes his hands trembled; he had steeled his will to control his hands, to keep them in line with the correct tempo. He groaned. He moved his lips.

The woman stared with horror at the images on the screen. She had taken the score on her lap to be able to read along. Did the pianist know that he was going to die? His contortions seemed to reflect this knowledge. He wormed himself into the music with his bloated body; he hunched his back in order to shut out all other reality—the lamps, the technicians, the clock. Against his better judgment he formed a shield against the world, an eggshell inside which he was alone with Bach. Meanwhile that intimate relationship was shot and recorded in image and sound so that the woman could watch it years later. An obscene spectacle from which you distance yourself by means of the viewing itself. A farce.

He started the twenty-fifth Variation, the dramatic climax of the entire work. An adagio. Gould took the tempo as slowly as possible; he could just about hold the lines in his head, all the misery was almost at a standstill.

This is despair, thought the woman, what I see is someone who knows and doesn't know at the same time, who is distraught with knowing, who tries to hide in the skimpily cut cloak of despair that Bach holds up for him. Here, stick your arms into it—I'll pull up the collar so that the coat fits perfectly around your shoulders. Now *play*.

He played. He had forgotten the spectators, the viewers, for as long as it lasted, and it seemed to last forever. The melody was lost, the foot had slipped from the pedal, and there was no longer any connection between the notes that, in Glenn Gould's head, were firmly connected. He floated high above the bottomless tragedy of this adagio; he built up nothing, demonstrated nothing, interpreted nothing. He was careful. With skinny fingers he pointed at the keyboard; fast, too fast, as if it were forbidden, he touched the keys, quick strokes like a bird's beak. No dynamic. No line. He worked deliberately at fragmentation until it was unrecognisable.

With small finger movements he tapped the keys one by one at a ten-centimetre distance from his face. No one should be allowed to see this. Gould, desperate, was screwing Bach.

She opened the lid of the grand piano and did not place it at the highest position—she didn't want a wide-open maw with all that sound tumbling out—but put it at the lowest, so that the strings could breathe freely and the sound was not locked in a closed box. Piano lamp on. Book open. The aria. G major. 'This is our song.' The woman placed her hands, the muscled hands with visible veins, in her lap, and looked at the notes.

Years ago she had once been the principal guest on a popular television programme. She was allowed to invite a few other guests and had asked a pianist friend who had just started to record the complete keyboard works of Bach on CD. The first CD had come out a short time before: the Goldberg Variations. Together they had discussed what he would play from it during the programme—something virtuoso, something difficult, something surprising? No. The aria. Something that appeals to everyone.

The daughter had come along and sat in the audience in the stands. She wore an orange velour top that had belonged to the woman. The daughter had contacted the technicians, the director, and the host of the programme because the following week the singer of her favourite songs would be a guest, and she wanted to be invited to that. The woman, the mother, sat at the side of the podium and watched how the pianist sat down, concentrated, and struck the first notes of the aria. An intent silence hung in the large factory hall that had been converted to a studio. She looked into the audience and saw the face of her daughter, warmly illuminated by the colour of her top. The small hands, the solid breasts, the narrow shoulders. The face.

A glimpse of shiny teeth behind slightly parted lips, wide-open eyes focused on the grand piano in the distance, hair thrown back. The light brushed against the delicate hairs at her temples. She sat still and listened as if she wanted to eat the music. She has a healthy appetite, thought the woman. Whether they are the special songs of the singer who will be standing here next week, or a masterpiece by Bach—the daughter experiences it without preconceptions and keeps what moves her without asking herself too many questions. She also had no need to be too critical—for that she was too young, or too kind, or not sufficiently embittered. In a bad performance she could still hear the beauty of the music; she generously overlooked all sorts of flaws. She certainly heard them—she knew exactly when someone sang off-key and why an interpretation was boring or affected. Good ears.

They were partially hidden by the smooth hair, the small, perfect ears of the daughter.

After the final measures she bent her upper body down to her thighs—the shoulder-length hair fell forward—then straightened up and, with a radiant smile, began to applaud.

Slowly, with difficulty, the woman lifted her arms. For a moment she leaned with both hands against the music rack as if she had to stop herself from crashing into the keys with her head. Then she straightened her back and moved the music so that Variation 1 stood exactly in the middle of the music rack. G major. The first dance.

Variation 1

Ate in a rush, hurriedly dumped the dirty dishes in the sink, put the boy in the pusher—if he walks by himself he stops everywhere, bending down inquisitively to inspect a dog turd, jumping up to pull elderberries from a bush. It's still light, no fiddling with coats. Windows closed, have the key?

The daughter dances in the front yard and sings softly to herself: 'Three geese in oat straw, sit there complaining.' She is wearing a full skirt with flounces, pink and white. Sturdy sandals on her feet. She turns her face to her mother and her brother, beaming expectantly. Are we going?

They run past the gardens at full speed. Behind the windows people are eating. Here and there someone is already doing dishes. The three of them sing at the top of their voices about the geese; the mother moves the pusher in wide zigzags over the pavement to the slow three-quarter time of the song. The little boy clasps his fists around the bar of the pusher and imitates an engine. The daughter holds onto the pusher with one hand and whirls along in the zigzags, singing.

They pass by familiar places. The tulip tree with its trimmed leaves. The front yard with the pond and the bridge across it for the postman. The dangerous dog behind an alarmingly low fence. They walk in a wide circle along the other side of the street. A small flight of steps with a wheelchair ramp—anything coming, car, bicycle? No, so race down, and on the other side of the street back up the ramp using the remaining speed. Now the bear falls out of the pusher, and the boy calls out. What a deep voice he has, unbelievable that such a bass sound can come from a three-year-old. They come to a halt and the girl skips back to pick up the lost bear. She wedges it carefully behind the broad back of her little brother, who mutters gratefully.

There is no wind. The scent of stock wafts from the gardens. Then the community centre comes into view, a grey building with a flat roof. It is located on a square where young trees were planted not very long ago, thin trunks with small crowns that let the light through. Children are coming from all directions, in groups, some accompanied by a father or a mother. The boy bellows enthusiastically to acquaintances and tries to stand up in his pusher. The daughter shows her skirt to a slightly older girl who nods in admiration. 'Really pretty.'

The mother manoeuvres the pusher past the wide open doors. She frees the boy who immediately starts running through the grey space, past the chairs that have been pushed against the walls, straight across the floor, over the grey linoleum. He carries the bear under his arm, firmly.

The folkdance group consists mostly of girls; the youngest are about six years old and the oldest are no more than nine. They are crowded together near the leader, a woman in her thirties with a long skirt and her hair in a braid down her back. The mother, distrustful of folkdance lovers and preservers of "folk culture", looks critically at the face of this teacher—no makeup, of course, but fortunately not healthy and rosy-cheeked. Instead, her face is rather pale, tired, but reviving with the children's interest.

The teacher fiddles with a large tape recorder. 'We are going to change,' she says, 'for the wooden shoe dance.' She takes bonnets and checked kerchiefs from a garbage bag.

'The wooden shoes, Mummy,' says the girl. She leans against the mother's knees for a moment, then sits down on the floor to take off her sandals. Barefoot, she walks to her brother, who stares in bewilderment at the dressing-up. She places her arm around his sturdy neck. 'When you're four, you'll get to do this too. That's pretty soon.'

The mother has taken the wooden shoes and the socks out of her bag. She dresses the boy in an old, bright red hunting jacket and puts his train conductor's cap on his head. She wants him to know that he is part of it too, even though he is not allowed to join in. Blaring, rhythmic dance music comes from the tape recorder.

'*With* your partner,' says the teacher, 'and *hands* on each other's *shoulders.*'

The daughter dances with the girl next to her. The teacher has put a bonnet on her head that ties with a bow under her chin. Black fabric with a small flower pattern. All her hair is covered by it, and the fabric ends in a point on her forehead. Her small, round girl's face is serious with intent. Her eyes are focused on the teacher; the right leg, with a black, decorated wooden shoe is slightly lifted for the first step.

The mother pulls the boy onto her lap. While they look at the girls who are spinning around, they clap along with the clatter of the wooden clogs. The children turn in a circle in pairs, let go of each other to fan out in a large circle, then dance sideways toward each other with arms akimbo, clack-clacking with their clogs.

Seeing how your own child moves in the world outside the family creates mixed feelings. It isn't right, you think, dancing takes place in the living room, as we used to do when she was a baby and I'd hold her on my arm, whirling through the room. Not with strangers, not led by someone who barely knows her. Is she armed? Strange children can call her names and tease; a new teacher can give stupid assignments. Is she able to say no, turn away? Will she become shy at the glance of another, will she no longer dare to dance, will she cry because she is uncomfortable and not used to all that? How can a child manage when things and people and music are different from the way they are at home? It is the mother's responsibility to prepare the child for hypocrisy: to be curious as well as alert, ready for dedication as well as mistrust. Has she done this adequately?

The daughter with the modest little bonnet dances. The mother sees how she smiles when, after a figure, she skips back to the girl next to her. She dances flawlessly to the beat. 'The other leg,' she says when her partner makes a mistake. At the next choreographed parting they wave quickly to each other before placing their hands back on their hips. They practise a new series of movements. Arms hooked together, spin around, stomp the outside foot. Stand still, other arm, go the other way, the other clog. How is it possible, the mother thinks, my daughter dances the wooden shoe dance, it just happens, and we are watching it.

Then it is suddenly finished. The children gather around the teacher to hand in their kerchiefs and their bonnets. I have to untie the bow, thinks the mother, and she almost gets up. Then she sees how the girl next to her daughter gently places her hand on her daughter's head; she says something; her lips move. She unties the bow and lifts the bonnet carefully from the daughter's head.

Seeing how the child gets along in the world, that she can enjoy herself and be involved in something. That she can bring about understanding and tenderness in people outside the family. That she is becoming an autonomous person, outside the walls of the home. The mother hides her face behind the back of the boy.

∞

Twenty-five years later, the mother, with pursed lips, looks at Variation 1.

'You'll play that in no time,' said a pianist friend. 'Go and practise it again; it's good for you.'

Ta-dah, she thought scornfully. Can you think scornfully? She can. Playing a dance, that graceful galumphing in three-quarter beat, was showing off. It did not become authentic unless you showed off extravagantly. First just the notes, without the pedal, slowly. That wasn't as easy as you'd think; it was more difficult than you'd expect. Runs alternated with arpeggios; the hand had to extend and then, suddenly, contract again. Annoying.

Her dissatisfaction with the physical, the technical problems—she made so many mistakes that she was afraid the errors would be imprinted—was combined with irritation at the childlike cheerfulness of this polonaise-like music. Memories assaulted her in fragments, with violent intensity. How she had sat behind her cello, facing her daughter, and played a rhythmic bass line under the lively dance that the girl played on her flute. It went naturally, the emphasis on the first beat, the barely noticeable wait at the end of the measure, as if they wavered, holding their breath for a moment before taking the step to the next one. They didn't need to talk about anything; the conversation took place solely through the music. One would play an improvised ornament, an articulation that was not written down, and the other would take it up. Spontaneously.

She shook her head as if she had washed her hair; the memories flew to all sides like drops of water. Variation 1. She played rigidly, controlled, a fraction slower than the obvious tempo. As she played, the music increasingly became a sturdy shell around a fiery core of anger. Under her hands the cheerfulness changed into something resembling cynicism. This first variation offered a choice: surrender to the infectious, naïve cheerfulness or distance oneself from it, with mistrust. She chose the latter. Her interpretation was a chilly polonaise, a cold commentary on the dance.

At the end of the piece, her hands moved toward each other, a simple scale in contrary motion, ending on the same key. It concluded. The face of the daughter appeared to her: six years old, eyes closed under the little black bonnet, surrendering to the gentle gesture of the girl next to her.

Filled with rage, the mother played the harsh, rigid polonaise.

Variation 2

You could let yourself be dazzled by an unconditional admiration for Bach, thought the woman. In that case the second variation was charming. Restful too, those two voices at the same time, like two violins with a cello under them. Three enthusiastic grey-haired amateurs could enjoy it together, before opening a bottle of Rhine wine.

She did it by herself. The upper voice somewhat stronger than the lower voice, the descending triads decrescendo, to avoid unwanted accents. The bass was sometimes staccato, and then again legato. The same melody lines continued, it resembled a canon. Soon another canon would follow, a real one, Variation 3. A variation in what respect?

As soon as the small hurdles had been cleared, she began to feel intensely bored. It was boring. It was so boring.

It was so terribly boring that while she was playing she could think of other things to her heart's content. For example, about the concept of boredom, its usefulness and necessity. There was something undeniably pleasant in boredom; it offered something to hold onto and kept us from confusion. Thanks to boredom things could be surprising—just think of that one sudden break in the clouds during a completely grey day. In a boring world you knew where you stood, and sometimes you needed that badly.

If people understood boredom they would not need to become excited and do strange, dangerous things. Is there an age for boredom? Do old people feel dull because there is nothing more, that's all? Teenagers don't think they are boring, but they experience the world as such to shield themselves from passion. If the young mother had to describe her life she would have called it boring, but she didn't experience it that way. It was only a word. Her day was monotonous, but there was a lot to experience in that one tone. And there was no time for boredom with small children at home.

Boring was a strange word that made her think of mooring and whoring, words that refer to connection and movement, but boring seemed so quiet and so alone. Perhaps boring was indeed a cover for indescribable, exciting events and thoughts. Actually, this music, too, sounded as if there was a secret hiding behind it. You caught a glimpse of it, your suspicion was strengthened rather than contradicted—until the extremely boring run of sixths and the stuffy final measure that drove all hope into the ground.

She pushed in the left pedal and repeated the second part softly, barely audibly, with a staccato bass. Still rather difficult to keep the sound so discreet, but it had to be done. She felt very reluctant to make too much sound in this variation.

∞

The daughter reached the age of twenty-seven. A young woman who had finished her studies the year before, but wary of taking the steps to adulthood. No boyfriend with whom she might want to have children, no house with a garden and a bicycle shed, no job that even resembled a career.

In the early morning she gets on her bicycle and rides to a traffic light on Ceintuurbaan where she is to meet an old friend. They have known each other since pre-school. Both of them work in large offices on the west side of the city. The temp agency placed them there; they didn't even know that something like that existed. They don't have a map of the city in their heads and cycle from one familiar place to the next: Concertgebouw, Haarlemmerpoort, Westerpark. From then on they search in the jungle of glass, steel, and stone. They refuse to look at a map; they don't want to know where they go every day; it's too awful, but it's only temporary.

On the way, they chat. From behind his glasses the young man looks sideways at his bicycling friend; he sees the movements of her eyes and her lips vaguely, as if through a poorly adjusted lens. He rides on her right side, next to her right hand that sometimes lets go of the handlebars to make gestures in the air.

'When I had my birthday last month, I treated everyone in the office to lollipops,' she says. 'Lollipops, they like that. One of the women bought glasses with a lollipop holder. We sit in a huge room with desks. Actually I've got zero to do, the same for the others. I think. Yet, busy-busy-busy. I have to prepare a big campaign: The New Logo. Busy for months. Meetings that I'm not allowed to attend, but they send me the report. By email. Also from the "Createam." And that logo will have to go on the cups in the cafeteria. It doesn't stop, there's no end to it. I have to take it seriously, otherwise it's pathetic, don't you think? But it makes no sense, I think. I don't even know what the former logo was, or the name of the place where I work.'

They fall silent. At a bus stop they turn off into the industrial park.

'One time I had to be examined for military service,' the young man says suddenly. 'It was some place around here; I had put the paper with the address in my pocket. I'd even left especially early. But it didn't work. I couldn't find it. Looked all morning. Then I just went back on the bus.'

'Those who really work here, they know it. They're attached to it! They know all the buildings! The people in my office have been working there for years. Every day it's the same, even the way they come in. When someone lower comes in later than someone higher up, they click their tongues and point to their watches. They're so different from what I'm used to that I haven't even got around to wondering whether they're nice. The manager of my department is a prick. "Didn't they teach you that at the u-ni-ver-si-ty," he says when I can't download an attachment. According to him, I have to pay him back some money because I didn't know that you were supposed to punch out at lunch. Those kinds of things, and they get worked up about them. World problems. I'll finish what I have to do in half an hour. Then I go and check what's on everyone's desks. What kind of shoes they're wearing. Who speaks to whom. Then I start emailing my friends to tell them about it. It's not allowed, but they all do it.

'Every day they're obsessed with these problems. When do we introduce the new rules for bicycle storage? Where are we going this year for our company outing? Shall we move the coffee break fifteen minutes? *There*, at that orange rubbish bin, that's where we have to turn left. And then you turn into the cross street in a moment.'

Her ponytail bounces up and down as she nods along with her words.

'This one man—I write the pieces for the company newsletter for him—he's very sweet. On weekends he stays in a Centre Parcs cottage with his wife and children.

Variation 2

When we had solidarity day—last week—we fled together on a tandem. We went cycling and then smoked cigarettes somewhere in the woods. You can talk with him, carry on a conversation—where you both talk about the same thing, I mean. Understand what the other is saying. I just don't understand the sense of humour of the others. I don't know what they like, except for the lollipops. How they can stand it in that large room full of world problems.'

They stop at the intersection.

'That prick, the one who wants me to pay back the hours, sits and complains every afternoon: "Oh, I'm so bored, tell a joke, do something funny." Then the whole office hides behind their screens. No one says anything. If he starts again this afternoon, I'll jump onto the table and start to sing. I'll have to figure out which song.

'In school I sometimes thought: this is the most boring thing on earth. Do you still remember how you simply couldn't keep your eyes open, how you just wanted to put your head down on the desk? This is even worse; this is deadly boring. It can't be worse.'

'And Solidarity day?'

'Well, the usual, in a circle, and then you have to let yourself fall with your eyes closed. Trusting they will catch you. And do a jigsaw puzzle together without talking.'

'Did it work?'

She reflects for a moment. Her calf muscles are tensed; she touches the footpath with the toe of her new grey sneaker.

"Actually, yes. Now that you ask. On the way back we had a flat tyre. Five of us were in the car. Taking the wheel off on the shoulder of the road, looking for the new wheel, screwing it on—it went practically by itself, smoothly. Almost without talking. I stood there and looked at it, from a distance. It was almost evening, the sun was setting and the traffic continued to drone on. I thought: what am I doing here? They change a wheel; I see their bare backs above their baggy trousers. I don't care about any of it, and yet I keep looking. I wasn't even annoyed. I looked; it was taking place slowly, like a slow-motion videotape.'

'We'll tackle it today! See you at five o'clock?'

The young man cycles off, raising his hand as he turns the corner without looking back.

I'm going to write really stuffy sentences, she thinks, for the internal booklet about the new rules for health and safety—long, boring sentences that keep repeating the same thing until the required number of words has been reached. Careful sentences that no one gets excited about, sentences that you could just as well not write. But I'll do it. Then I'll email my friends that I'm going to let it all hang out this weekend and I'll ask who wants to join in.

She looks over her shoulder to check if she can cross the road and then takes off to cycle to her office. More than two hours to go until the coffee break.

Variation 3, canon at the unison

Symbiosis. That word best expressed how the woman felt when she carried the daughter inside her body. Sharing blood circulation, temperature regulation, moisture management. Feeling each other's movements and changes of position and, barely aware, take that into account. Now I take care of my child, the woman had thought, better and more naturally than I will ever be able to later. And easier, it goes by itself. We sing the same song, in unison. If only it could stay like that.

Is birth also something that happens twice? You bear a child: it is a tragedy. And then, around twenty years later, you cast the now adult young woman halfheartedly out of the parental home: a farce. In the meantime, the melody lines have started to diverge, and a song in perfect unison has disappeared long ago. How does it actually happen, how can it be that you want to remain close to each other and yet drift apart more and more?

Of course, the gynaecologist was to blame, an annoying, arrogant locum who replaced her trusted doctor. He pulled the child out of her with force. Against her will. Suddenly the delivery room with the intimidating instruments seemed not lifesaving but destructive—the glaring light a warning about what it was like in the world. The woman, already worn out from hours of pain and agitation, had changed her mind and did not want to give birth. The child would be better off inside her.

'It's just like the lid of a jam pot,' the gynaecologist said as he waved a silver object. 'I place it against the head, we create a vacuum, and I pull your child out. You must co-operate because it has to happen now.'

In her mind she had seen a table set for breakfast in a country house in the Veluwe area. Bone napkin rings and silver lids on the jam jars, with a notch in them for a long spoon. The gynaecologist as a small but already totally stuck-up little boy, pushed up to the table in a high chair. Co-operate, never. He made the notch in *her*, just like that, without anaesthesia, with scissors. Dazed and defeated she had undergone everything. In the end she was convinced that she would die on the delivery table. It was as it should be; go ahead, she thought. The child doesn't want to, I don't want to—and yet it is happening.

Did she feel recognition when the child was placed at her breast? No, it was instead a natural reunion. They were together again after a dismal interlude in which outsiders had tried to separate them. Now the daughter was hurting, and she, the mother, was hurting. She held the small baby firmly and tried to retrieve the common rhythm. She was furious at the doctor, at the nurses, even at the father. At everyone who had felt that this expulsion was normal and inevitable. You might think that she would reproach the child, since it was the cause of all the fear and pain, but that wasn't so. The baby, with the red, round suction imprint on her skull was the only thing she could hold onto, the only being that she trusted in that hellish room. The baby opened its eyes and looked at her. Yes, the mother thought, yes, you.

Temperature differences, various cloths, spray cans with disinfecting liquids squeeze between mother and child. Hunger and satiety alternate; that which was natural no longer exists, it no longer comes about naturally, instead an effort has to be made to reach this condition. This condition is no longer a permanent characteristic of the dual oneness but is displaced by other conditions where the baby lies in the bassinet by herself and the mother stands sobbing in the shower. When the baby cries, efforts to recover the dual oneness don't succeed. Despite holding, rocking and singing, the discontent lingers, the baby turns red in the face and loud protest keeps flowing from the small, toothless mouth. A new disquiet appears: is everything going all right? Is she drinking enough, is she gaining weight, is her colour all right, and what about her temperature? Doctors and visiting nurses are meddling in what had been hers alone; newspaper articles and pharmacists give advice that she even listens to. It's irritating. It's irritating, but she gets used to it. The shift becomes normal. An apple cut in half, she thinks, and both halves, shifted a fraction, have been pressed together again. For the most part we understand each other quite well, but there are unguarded edges where you're suddenly alone and at a loss.

Peace sets in after a few weeks. The small distance makes it possible to smile at each other. The child squeezes her eyes into slits and opens her mouth wide into a sweet smile. The baby stops crying as soon as she hears the woman's voice. The child is adjusting to the world. This idea sometimes terrifies the woman. What I do, how I am, becomes a standard for her. That's how it is, thinks the baby. Well, she doesn't think yet, but she feels, she perceives and remembers. And what she perceives is almost completely determined by the mother.

How it smells in the house, what kind of music is heard, the length of the wait for a clean nappy. Really scary.

The child seems to help her because she is open with her feelings, expressing clearly both her happiness and her displeasure with everything that happens. A game begins between the two who once were one. The child follows the mother with enormous concentration and reacts to every fluctuation in her voice, to every gesture. Entranced, the mother looks at the child and focuses on every movement, every change in the direction of her gaze.

The mother accompanies the entry of the world into the child's perception with a constant stream of words. The child assures the mother of her trust, her cooperation, by her small, quick respiration during the night. That's how it is, thinks the woman, a gap, a small gap has appeared, and we are used to it. The gap will become deeper and larger, that is unavoidable. The capacity to adjust will be stretched to the utmost. The way we can now hold each other across the gap, with sounds and gazes—that is how, later on, we will be able to find ways to reach each other across greater depths.

It is night. The woman has fed and changed the child. The baby girl lies with her head on the shoulder of the mother who presses the satisfied, supple little body against her breast. How seamlessly, how easily a very young child adjusts to the mother's body. She inhales the daughter's smell and carries her child to the open window. Gently she rocks back and forth and sings about the stars, the black sky, the moon. The baby sleeps.

∞

A canon consists of two, three, or more voices, all of which sing the same melody but start at different times. The form resembles a fugue but is much less free. Of course the voices of

Variation 3, canon at the unison

the fugue repeat each other, the theme and the countersubject, but between these they go their own way. A voice of the fugue is fanciful and whimsical; suddenly it sings the theme twice as fast or slowly, or upside-down, however it works out. It can start the theme forcefully but then suddenly drop it to go and sing something else. But not so the voice of the canon. That voice is tied to the melody, it goes as fast or as slowly as the time signature, and does not stray.

Bach, the very greatest fugue writer, was crazy about canons. The stricter the rules, the more he enjoyed himself. A canon was a challenge that made him feel cheerful rather than disheartened. He composed canons in which voices in contrary motion sang their answer, or in which a reply came from another interval, or both. As many voices as he wanted, so that the canon danced in full swing into the ears of listeners as a wild swarm of notes. Only he himself could still distinguish the voices.

The woman knew that it is impossible to hear two things at the same time, according to the physiology of the senses. You thought that you heard two voices sing at the same time, but you went imperceptibly, and with lightning speed, from one voice to the other. What presented itself as something smooth was a feverish, always slightly halting leap in the reality of the unconscious. You could practise it; it was a part of your work as a pianist. From a harmonious humming, you could, after a certain amount of time, distinguish four notes, which together formed a chord that you could name. Dominant seventh chord. A 6/4 chord with an added second. Diminished. Nameless. Just as the immobile harmonies could be analysed and named, in the same way the canon voices could also be disentangled. Work. Something that could be learned.

Bach had restrained himself with the canons from the Goldberg Variations and restricted himself to only two voices, an enormous constraint that lent itself to unbridled mastery. The first one now stood on the rack, a dreamlike song that pulled its identical twin sister behind it. In every bar you heard the repetition of the previous one; the new grew spontaneously out of the old, and everything occurred twice. Nothing was left of the aria—the theme on which this canon forms the third variation—except the harmonic scheme, and you barely paid attention to that when you were busy sorting out the two voices. You played both of them with the same hand, a *tour de force*. In your head, in your thinking, you pulled the two voices apart and, in time, could distinguish them everywhere; in your body, in your muscle memory. Together they formed a whole. You used the same fingers now for one and then again for the other voice. Learning the movements took up all your concentration for quite some time.

But there was more. Under the tissue of the voices penetrating each other, a dark singing was perceptible: a bass steadily striding along that indicated the harmonic origin, the aria. As the canon progressed, this bass part appeared increasingly, in ever shorter notes he sang along with the higher voices. It was impossible to imagine life without him; he took care of what was needed and became an essential part of the whole.

∞

The father meets the child nine months after the mother. There is a lag. There is a difference because the experience of physical oneness will remain foreign to him. From time to time during these months the father feels the daughter's heel kicking against the mother's abdominal wall; he sees how the belly grows from week to week—a phenomenon that can only be observed from a distance, however small—just as he will in the end observe the violent delivery.

Variation 3, canon at the unison

The father drives back and forth to the hospital. He buys a giant bouquet with blue flowers. He calls friends and relations. He does the first errands when mother and child have come home with him. He is there when the child feeds. For him the child is a new person, someone who has joined them. He is startled when he hears her breathing at night. There are three of us! It takes him by surprise.

Slowly a connection develops. The father lifts the child out of the bassinet. The baby smells a new, another scent and hears a deeper voice. When the father blows his nose, trumpeting above the bassinet, she startles awake, crying. Soon she knows: that's how it is, he sounds like that; he belongs.

The bass climbs ever closer against both canon voices. Impossible to imagine life without him.

Variation 4

Early in the morning the father drives up. The large family car squeezes into the narrow street where the daughter lives. Is she already standing in the doorway with suitcase and backpack? The light grey façade glistens in the sun. A window on the third floor bangs shut. The father parks the car in an empty disabled parking space across from the door. His face looks relaxed and cheerful; he is going to take his daughter to Schiphol Airport for her week's holiday in Italy. First pick up her two travel companions at Amstel Station—they're already waiting, brightly coloured bags at their feet, sunglasses on their noses. In the car, words zip back and forth like ping-pong balls between the three women. They are close to thirty, but right now they're behaving like young girls. They are carrying with them thick stacks of gossip magazines, they have new bikinis and shiny tank tops in their luggage; they play *Charlie's Angels*, whatever that is.

The father asks if they're sure the rental car is waiting for them, who's going to drive across the Apennines at night, and whether they will drink beforehand? Well, start right away with some whiskey or cocktails—what is it you drink there, what's it called, red and bitter, Campari!—tipsy across those mountains, of course.

'Don't worry, Dad,' says the daughter who doesn't have a driver's licence, 'we won't drink anything. I'll read the map. We're adults, remember.'

She waves an ancient road map of Italy. 'Mum gave me this. To see where we were before; it's marked. Soon I'll see it all again.'

One of them has a professional camera to record everything; the other is calling on a tiny telephone. The daughter's cell phone rings. She is always in conversation, thinks the father. Her friends know how to find her anywhere, long before mobile phones existed. She'd come on her bike to her parents' house to have a good meal or to study undisturbed; before she has even taken off her coat, the phone rings. For her.

'Yes, I have the money. *And* my passport. We're now driving past McDonald's. I'll call you when we board!'

'It was Mum.' She puts the telephone in her bag, a small childish-looking straw basket. 'I have to vomit. I've got travel nerves.' The girlfriends laugh.

At the airport the father helps load all the suitcases and bags on a cart.

'Shit, what a line!' They join the long line of people snaking in front of the check-in counter and straight away begin to comment on their fellow travellers, giving them names, destinations, biographies.

The father remains standing behind the silver line at the passport control; he watches how his child jokes with the security guard, how she—nervous all the same, as if she could be caught at anything at all—steps almost timidly through the metal detector and jumps for joy when the alarm doesn't go off. Then all three of them are done; they wave and point with exaggerated gestures at the liquor store; they double over with laughter about nothing; the daughter rummages with both hands in her bag, boarding pass lost, already, oh no, thank God in her pants' pocket—the girlfriends each throw an arm around her, and the father sees them disappear; sees his daughter being carried off to pleasure palaces, to crowded beaches, to discos and trattorias, to the house or the kitchen or the bed of some Italian friend whom she met last year. The last thing that he sees of his child is her girl's profile, open mouth, a quick movement of the head that makes her hair fan out in the air, like in a television ad, a laugh…

'It was still there! The lake where we were that time, where they sold forty kinds of ice cream! That's where we stopped. I recognised it. We wanted to swim then, but you wouldn't let us. There was going to be a thunderstorm, remember?'

'You were twelve,' says the mother. 'It was fifteen years ago. How nice that you've seen it again.'

The father and mother drive through northern Germany to Sweden, the country where the father grew up; the child drives in a southern direction on the other side of Europe; they are further and further apart. In the two cars, the mother and the daughter each sit with a telephone at their ear, shouting against the notion of distance.

In Italy it's a party every day; the girls do as they please. They are staying with a friend of the daughter.

'He thinks that we should do the cooking, Mum! Women are supposed to do that, he says. We want to eat out. Then he gets angry.'

Afternoons on the overcrowded beach, conversations, jokes. Nights in the fragrant garden, cigarettes, wine.

'I've bought fantastic shoes, you'll see them when I join you. And new sunglasses. Haven't read a thing. Yesterday I

Variation 4

sang in the restaurant—there was a band. Just went up to them and asked which numbers they knew. The drummer spoke a little English. It went very well. Now I'm really hung over.'

The mother listens for traces of sadness in the daughter's voice; the holiday with her girlfriends is instead of a cancelled trip with her boyfriend. Decisions were made in a huge rush: relationship ended, take it or leave it, right away a consolation trip, quick, quick. A girlfriend takes you in when you are too sad to sleep alone; you can get in bed with her—she places a sick bowl next to you on the floor. A girlfriend is forever. She goes with you when you have to be tested at that sinister STD clinic; you support her when her parents are getting a divorce. Girlfriends are the canvas on which you embroider your life. Certainty.

All three are exhausted by a year of being adults after finishing their studies—they know it's difficult to grow up and are reluctant to do so. Now everything will be different; in between the demands and exhortations of their Italian host, they talk about it in the garden as they drink Italian wine. That terrible office job has got to go; the daughter is seriously considering becoming a teacher and will be a substitute for half a year to see if she can do it.

Of course you can, thinks the mother, it's made for you; the pupils will adore you. She says nothing. Don't try to influence, don't know better, bite your lip, and close your mouth.

'It was evening,' says the daughter, 'we were sitting on the beach; it was still very warm, but most people had gone home; we sat there alone and looked at the sea. It was quiet. My hair was sticky with salt; I pulled it back into a bun. I thought: from now on I'll handle everything properly. Keep my paperwork up to date. Ask for a tax refund. Pay bills. Play the oboe in the orchestra. Answer letters. Clean the house.

Wash my clothes on time. I said it out loud; they nearly died laughing. But I'm going to do it.'

She said that they took photos, huge numbers of photos—she looked at the photographer through her legs; she put on her silly hat, tried ten different sunglasses, posed as dejected, as indifferent, as elated. 'And as myself.'

After the connection is broken, the mother places the telephone in her lap and leans back. In her mind she sees the three women, how they react wittily to each other, how they challenge and protect each other, how they skip from one subject to the other, make incomprehensible comments on everything they encounter—their secret language, their speed, their cohesion. She pities the home-loving Italian who can whistle for his homemade meals. She can hardly wait to see her daughter again, curses the car that carries her the wrong way. Only two more weeks—then she can see the photos.

∞

What an odd variation, this fourth one, thought the woman. A storm of short motifs, a chaos of sharply broken chords. Against each other, interrupting or affirming each other, questioning or triumphant—a cacophony of related voices. The notes looked simple, but that was an illusion. The longer she slaved away at it, the more difficult it became to emphasise every small fragment. It didn't work at all—it was simply too much. The mood seemed too dance-like, and at a moderate tempo it soon sounded pedantic. In a quick tempo it immediately fell apart, a sloppily dashed-off piece of music whose essence escaped you.

It is strange to me, thought the woman, I don't follow it well; I don't really feel it. Why all that galumphing, rustic or courtly, no matter how you want to play it? What is it about? Very clever how the composer inverts and interweaves everything and still follows the required melodic line, everything in a single idiom—but it drives you crazy, and it carries you into the unintelligible. It made her think of inadvertently overheard conversations in a restaurant, in a streetcar, or perhaps on the beach. A raised voice, another that interrupted loudly, a buzz of voices alternating with distinct statements. Too chaotic to understand clearly. Accept it, she thought, just try first to get those notes right.

She tried to control the tempo, rather too slow than too fast; she tried to play the accented parts of the bars more strongly than the unaccented parts—the piece itself was such an accumulation of accented notes. She tried to do justice to the short variation without understanding it fully. The efforts made her feel sad. She was playing something that was over for good, something that she would never really be able to get back. She would never again be able to feel the way this piece sounded.

And yet it existed. The notes stood in front of her on the rack and became sound under her hands. The measures grouped themselves four by four. A forceful pronouncement, a whispered answer. In this way a kind of line did come about and it seemed as though she had mastery over it, an "interpretation," the result of a train of thought. All bogus, of course. Musical hyperbole. She didn't understand it at all, and the only thought that the piece evoked in her was: mournful, sad, futile.

This gets me nowhere at all, she thought with sudden anger. How far should I go? Can I ever play something that I haven't analysed to bits? I thought so.

The "interpretation" continued to wobble. One day sure and triumphant, the following day it could sound hesitant and sorrowful. Nothing to be done about it, that's how it was. With the pencil she wrote in her notebook what the variation reminded her of: fragments of conversation zipping between three young women on the beach in Italy, backed up by a bass voice that put forward predictable clichés—because he was uncertain in the language, because he didn't know the women well? There was one who sang along with him from time to time, so that he wouldn't feel completely excluded. It was the daughter, who always stood up for victims of ostracism and harassment, who possessed a boundless reserve of empathy.

The woman followed her voice, which sometimes joined in the girlfriends' discussion and at other times adjusted itself to the grumpy, slightly angry host. Beach, she wrote down, a windless evening at the beach. The conversations die down.

Variation 5

Ah, the fifth! Actually the second "virtuoso" piece in which the arms crossed and your thoughts also got mixed up if you didn't watch out. It would become increasingly worse further on in these Goldberg Variations. Bach had a solid build, even a pretty heavy paunch according to some depictions; how did he manage that crossed hands technique? On the other hand, he had no breasts—that made a difference. He was muscular and dexterous; the woman had read that he could play outrageously difficult melodies with his feet on the organ pedal.

The desire to get closer to Bach led to a passion for reading. In a way the result was mixed. The fact that Bach had read Cicero's orations in Latin at school created an unexpected bond because the woman had also done that, in high school. But the reports about Bach's virtuoso keyboard technique made her feel alienated. The woman did not have that talent. She had to fight for it, day after day. She had to keep up the command of a piece conscientiously and regularly, under penalty of loss. If she didn't manage it, then she had to start all over again. It was like the Roman Empire. If you did not constantly guard the conquered provinces, you would lose them; if the conquered territory became too large, your army would be too small in the long run. Bach was a powerful emperor.

Before he composed the Goldberg Variations, Bach had seen scores by Scarlatti. The techniques used by the composer—enormous leaps, crossed arms—inspired Bach. He imitated them; he used them for his own purposes. The woman was intensely grateful that Bach had not adopted the technique of lightning-quick repeating notes. Perhaps he thought it was a sign of musical poverty, perhaps the keyboard instruments in his house did not lend themselves to it? Anyway, she thought it was a lucky break. It was already complicated enough.

She started by here and there shifting the parts from one hand to the other, with Kirkpatrick as guide. She began to enjoy it, the way the voices tumbled over each other so nicely, played around each other solicitously, adjusted without urging to the harmonic scheme while experiencing their own adventures. She found the ornaments difficult; they went well only if she thought ahead, toward the solution. It was a game, a lively, contented game between two clear voices.

'Well. You're going to get a brother or a sister,' says the gynaecologist.

'Baby.' The girl stands up straight in front of his desk and looks at him across the overflowing desktop. The mother climbs onto the examination table, laborious and ponderous; it is a warm summer, and she is in her eighth month. She flips up her loose-fitting dress, and the belly is displayed in its taut smoothness under the light of the fluorescent lamp. The doctor looks, palpates, picks up a long, wooden horn that he places against the belly. He holds the tip against his ear. He closes his eyes.

'Do you want to hear it too?' He pulls a chair to the examination table and lifts the little girl onto it. She actually lets herself be lifted. She grasps the auscultation tube. She, too, closes her eyes. The mother holds her breath. I'll deliver only if he is on call, she thinks. No more jam pot lids. The daughter smiles.

'I think the baby has a watch,' she says.

On the way back, in the car, they sing the song of the big and small clocks. Tick-tock, tick-tock, tick-tock.

The birth of the second child affects the very foundations of the first one. There is nothing the mother fears more. Despite the disastrous first delivery, she gives barely a thought to the birth of this new child. She thinks up ways to prevent the older one from feeling pushed from her place and from thinking: I wasn't good enough and that's why they got another child. The mother withdraws the daughter's playgroup registration because it is not good to take her elsewhere at the very moment that the new child has arrived. The mother busies herself with a baby doll and a doll's bassinet, storybooks about new babies, baby bottles, nappies. She wants to console and heal, before there is even a question of a wound.

In the hospital she pulls the daughter close to her on the high bed and holds her tight. The scent of a two-and-a-half-year-old girl: straw-like, sweet, overwhelming. Together they look at the glass box where the little brother is sleeping.

Once at home, the new order begins. Feedings, with the son at the breast, and the daughter, busily bottle-feeding her doll between her legs. Reading, with the daughter nestled against her, the son exhausted and sated against her shoulder. Washing, changing, lugging warm water and dirty nappies.

With the daughter on her lap, sit for hours on end in front of the spinning washing machine and identify whose clothes are tumbling around. Put the baby in his bassinet and then quickly go downstairs, with the daughter, to play, read books, sing, finally together again. She looks pale, thinks the mother, she is shaken. I'll give her a baby bottle; she may lie in the pram, she may pee in her nappies as much as she wants. She doesn't have to be big, there will always be time for that when she feels like it. How will this work? I have harmed her.

Everything goes as a matter of course. The mother stands there and looks on when the children find each other. His first smile is for the sister; he starts bouncing with delight in his baby seat when he hears her voice; she sits down on top of him when he lies on the sofa—he doesn't protest but instead crows with joy. He lies in the cart that she pulls with her tricycle, and she rides around and around in the room with him. At night his bassinet stands next to her child's bed with rails. When he wakes up, she sings for him; when he screams, she goes to the mother to ask for food; when he spreads the poo from his nappy everywhere, she encourages him.

They play house in the small sandbox near the terrace. She adapts her game brilliantly to his whims. 'Father is going to a rehearsal,' she says when he crawls away.

Every evening they sit together in their bath. She wants him to be there when they sing songs at the piano. When he is taking his afternoon nap upstairs, she climbs up the stairs: 'Just to check if he's really there.'

She turns four; there is a children's party with a game of drop the hanky and bobbing for apples. The next day she goes to nursery school. Everything that happens there is meticulously repeated and discussed on her return home. The daughter and the girl next door tell the boy what they've done at school, sit with him in a circle for sharing time, and teach him new songs. At lunchtime the mother walks to school with him; self-confident, he runs across the schoolyard, the bear and the rabbit clasped tightly in his arms, his head wrapped in a red balaclava to prevent ear infections. He can't wait and roars with excitement when the bell rings. There she comes, his sister, her little face bursts into a wide smile and she rushes to him.

They go shopping in the shopping centre near the newly opened metro stop. Even in the supermarket you can, from time to time, hear the deep hum of onrushing and departing trains. The closing of the car doors is preceded by an ascending arpeggio, a piercing sound that produces a strange excitement. They should change that, thinks the mother, much too annoying; in the long run people won't be able to stand it.

On the occasion of the opening she had gone with the children to look at the metro platforms, they had stood expectantly, hand in hand, on the escalator. The rails with their deadly electrical charge lay three feet below the platform. No gate, no fencing. She had held the children's hands much too tightly. When the train finally arrived, it was filled with Saint Nicholas's helpers, Black Peters, who began to toss spice nuts on the platform. Sometime soon they should take a ride to the city. Here, in the suburbs, the track ran high above the ground on impressive columns, but further down the train tunnelled into the ground. Different arrangements, the same song.

The mother packs up the groceries. Oranges, milk bottles, imitation chocolate bars. She struggles, two bags in each hand, through the crowd to the exit. The daughter walks on her right, her hand through a bag handle. The son? The mother tries to look across the store, shuts out everything except the image of a solid little boy with a red cap. Even near the shelves with cookies and candy no one matches that image. Her heart drops straight through her body. Back outside, peering around, searching, calling out. Running around and asking: 'Have you seen a little boy with a red cap?' People shake their heads with incomprehension and disapproval.

The daughter pulls on her arm. 'Mummy, the metro!'

An about-face. Past the chemist's, the liquor store, the lamp display, buckets with brightly coloured flowers. The mother thinks of the platforms that slip into the abyss without warning. Jets of flame, cutting wheels.

One hundred, two hundred, four hundred metres. She pushes people aside brusquely, pulls the girl wildly behind her. A class of screaming children has just come off the escalator; they run every which way, snatch each other's school bags and bump into everything. Mother and daughter struggle though the unruly group and then suddenly stand in front of a deserted space, paved with wet bricks. Fifty metres from them, a child wearing a red balaclava stands at the foot of the escalator and carefully tries to put his boot on the lowest tread.

The mother sits in the hall, next to the door of the children's room.

'Again, again!' the boy mumbles.

The girl sings: 'There was a boy who wanted to go on the metro, but he was afraid of the escalator, and then there came a dragon!' She stresses "afraid" and "dragon" long and theatrically.

'Again!'

The mother hears him sigh contentedly while his sister sings of his adventures in a bright, clear voice.

Variation 6, canon at the second

'What are you going to be when you grow up?' asks the father.

The girl looks at her mother and tries, just like her, to pull her legs up under her on the couch.

'A mummy, of course.'

Surprised, the mother watches how her children choose their activities and with whom they identify in their play. Actually, she doesn't want to believe what she sees. In the family the division of labour of previous generations has been abandoned; the father and the mother both have visible and serious work, with obligations and preparations that have to be carried out at home. From time to time people come into the home to take care of the children: babysitters, sometimes a man and sometimes a woman. The father cooks at least as often as the mother.

During play the girl decorates the imagined house and the boy goes out and returns like a hero to be fed by her with homemade cake. During their play the girl slides her feet into the mother's old shoes with pointy stiletto heels, and the boy equips himself with sword and shield. Any buses and tractors that the girl receives as presents lay idle in the toy box until the boy lays claim to them.

They notice the concealed things, thinks the mother. They see that the father builds the fire in the fireplace of the summer cottage; they see that I fold the laundry, write detailed instructions for the babysitter, do the shopping for the whole week. Fathers forget the shampoo and the scouring pads. They see that I don't pay attention to the rubbish bin, that I leave it to him. But why does she want to adorn her face with mascara and lipstick while I put on makeup at most once a year?

When the boy puts on his sister's birthday dress and stands big and proud in front of the mirror, the mother and daughter smile pityingly. As soon as he dresses up as the strongest man in the world, they sound a lot more enthusiastic. In their bath the daughter says that she can later on have a baby, in her stomach. The boy's face clouds with envy.

'Me too!' he roars.

'No, that won't work. But you'll get a beard.'

Both children are able to take care of something, but they have a different notion of care. The girl feeds, washes and dresses her dolls, sings to them, and tells them stories. She combs the hair of the doll that has hair. The boy has the mother tightly wrap both of his animals, the bear and the rabbit, in stinking rags that are never allowed to be washed and then takes them everywhere—playgroup, ice rink, toilet. Most of the time he sticks one animal under each arm. When he needs his hands, both animals are close together in his backpack.

Both children want the mother's clothes. For the boy there is soon an end to that; he wants them for a time because he

Variation 6, canon at the second

admires his sister, but he leaves the scarves and the bras aside as soon as cranes and guns are at hand. For the girl it is different. Her interest in the mother's clothes continues. Of course she has objections to the mother when, in the second grade, she has a young, beautiful teacher with a perfect hairdo, but she still regularly opens the trunk with clothes from bygone days. When the daughter is around fifteen, she starts moving these clothes to her own wardrobe. The mother is touched when the daughter enters in *her* old denim jacket, when the daughter dresses up for the school party in *her* favourite old dress.

The daughter will take the mother's clothes with her when she leaves home. She will wear these clothes and will let herself be admired by her girlfriends.

Later, later the mother will in turn store the daughter's T-shirts and jumpers, carefully folded, in her wardrobe. There comes a time that the mother leaves the house in the leather jacket, thinking of the daughter's narrow hands that lay, curled up like small animals, in the pockets of her jacket.

∞

The canon at the second was an unpretentious tune, rippling gently in a three-part cadence. After the very first measure, the second voice joined the first; it sounded the same but different—younger, perhaps brighter—because it started on the next step of the scale. The voices stayed close together, twisted together, and imitated each other in an almost ridiculous manner.

The woman tried to play the voice that started later more softly than the first one so that you could hear the model and then its echo. Without exactly knowing how it happened, the plan always failed, and the imitator gradually became more prominent than the model. No matter how she handled and shifted the dynamic of the voices, the intense interaction of the almost identical songs remained constant.

Whether she leads or I, thought the mother, is of no importance. It changes. What is important is that we move to the same beat. What counts is that the song of one person gets its depth from the song of the other. In time, she no longer tried to do her best to let the voice leading be heard exactly, but intentionally let the notes mingle into a constantly revolving cloud of sounds in which the different sounds blended together completely.

Variation 7, al tempo di giga

The woman had always considered Variation 7 an island of clarity that in its simplicity rose above a sea of more complicated constructions. A sweet two-part song in 6/8 time that she had played gladly and often for the children. The bass was not really a bass but a fully-fledged voice singing along that carried the theme just as often as the descant. A siciliano, not too fast, played so liltingly that ears and brain could rest for a moment. It reminded her of a siciliano part in Brahms' beautiful Haydn Variations that she used to play with a friend, on two grand pianos. She thought of the countless sicilianos in Bach suites and in recorder instruction books.

It was never as you thought. There was always an expert who threw a spanner in the works, grumpy Kirkpatrick or another sanctimonious professor who knew better. The original manuscript said "al tempo dal giga" above that Variation and was there in one handwritten manuscript but not in the next, and it was not clear either whether it was Bach's own handwriting or his wife's, his son's, or his pupil's. But doubt was sown, and a choice had to be made between pastoral and intense. If she chose the gigue tempo, the piece would lose its calm because a gigue moved faster, sounded harsher and more purposeful than a siciliano. The ornaments would immediately have a virtuoso character instead of the sweet dreaminess they had now. The superb ascending runs to the high notes would sound brilliant rather than wistful.

The woman realised that you had to believe in an interpretation; otherwise it would not work. Could she believe in the directions of an unknown scholar? In case of doubt, suspending action is the proper answer. Close that book!

∞

The chandeliers in the large hall of the Concertgebouw consist of thousands of pieces of cut glass and look like breasts hanging down. They scatter the light and create a pleasant, warm mood. The mother points out the giant fittings. From their seats behind the stage, the three of them look into the hall where people are looking for their seats and are chatting with each other, excited with expectation, with neatly done hair and elegant clothes.

'It's a party, isn't it, Mum?' says the daughter. She rubs her body against the mother. She is wearing a floral summer dress with tights and winter boots. The boy has put on his warm-ups; he peers with concentration at the stage where the orchestra librarian is placing scores on the music stands. One by one the musicians appear with their instruments. The concertmaster bends over the centrally placed harpsichord and repeats the A. For a moment the single note floats in space, then it is submerged in a buzzing swarm of sound. They see the string players busily move their bows across the strings but can't hear any specific notes. From time to time, a wind player's A can be distinguished in the enormous buzz. When everyone has tuned, it is quiet.

'Here!' says the boy in his deep voice.

'He isn't looking,' says his sister. 'He's still talking.'

Behind the front row music stand the father is chatting with a colleague. The mother and the children see them from behind, how the backs in their black coats bend over the cellos, how the two men tune their lowest strings and smile at each other approvingly.

The whole orchestra stands up when the conductor comes down the stairs. The applause washes in wild waves from the audience to the stage. The conductor bows, turns toward the orchestra, lifts his hands and waits. The daughter nudges the mother and hunches her small shoulders in happy excitement. The boy pulls himself up as high as possible in his chair and continues looking intently at the father. His agitation is tangible, at least for the mother. She puts her arm round him but he shakes it off. The silence in the hall is complete; the audience holds its breath; the conductor waits another moment—and then gives the downbeat for the start.

"PAPA!" the boy bellows. Behind him an older gentleman sniffs indignantly. The conductor lowers his arms. The audience is in confusion, then bursts out laughing. Just look, thinks the mother, we're sitting *here*, just wave. The father turns around, finds his family in the higher seats, and waves with his bow. He shrugs his shoulders apologetically at the conductor, who smiles kindly.

The fourth Brandenburg Concerto has everything that a child desires: tempo, colour, melodies that keep returning in one form or the other. Recognition and surprise alternate. Next to the conductor, at the front of the stage, the solo violinist and the two recorder players are passionately playing their parts in a well-chosen tempo that manages to combine gravity with a dance-like character. The children listen entranced, both of them.

No one in the audience coughs during the solemn silence before the andante. Then the recorders soar with their woody, almost too direct sound, in a dramatic dialogue. A statement, an echo, a continuation. The woman thinks: G major, E minor; it will soon end on the dominant; then that strange fugue finale with the daredevil violin solo; but first this, now this. The words disappear and there is only sound, only line.

The girl is crying. The mother feels the child's body shake; startled, she looks next to her and sees eyes squeezed shut, tears, and snot. She pulls the child on her lap and wraps her arms around her. Gasping sobs are smothered in that warm embrace. She places her mouth against the daughter's ear and whispers: 'What's the matter? Are you hurt?'

The girl leans her head against the mother's shoulder.

'Are you sick? Just tell me.'

The girl sighs: 'Mummy, it's too beautiful.'

This was the start—during a Christmas matinee in the Concertgebouw—of her love for the recorder. The mother delights in the purchase of the modest instrument and the paraphernalia: oil to grease the unprotected wood; a giant size pipe cleaner to keep the insides clean; a bright case to store the flute. A slightly stale air always hung around recorders that reminded you of stuffy living rooms and of food that had been kept too long. The daughter plays and collects songs in a folder.

'Shouldn't she have a real instrument,' says the father. 'She is so musical; shouldn't she learn to play the piano or a string instrument?'

Well, thinks the mother, if she wants that, we'll notice. Here at home she hears piano and string sounds all day long, but she clearly longs for something different, a sound that

Variation 7, al tempo di giga

we don't know, whose lure we don't understand. Because she loves that sound so seriously, we should let that happen. Perhaps we have learned to laugh at the recorder, but we shouldn't pass this habit on to our children. Secretly, the mother holds the recorder dear because when she was young it had given her access to music, and she sees with joy how the daughter treads that path—earlier, more innocently, openly. Interfering in this process is unthinkable.

She plays duets with the daughter. She goes to music school performances and sobs in her handkerchief when the daughter plays a solo. The girl is soon chosen by the teacher to play in a quartet. She is the youngest but plays the first part with flair. Extra rehearsals, a new folder for the quartet parts, concerts in the home for the aged in the district. 'All grandmas,' says the daughter. 'They tried to sing along, but it didn't work. We got flowers and cake.'

Nothing remains unchanged. The quartet girlfriends go to high school, they get breasts and boyfriends and weekend jobs at the bakery. Soon the daughter too will be absorbed by life outside the music school. She isn't quite there yet, but the changing moods of approaching adolescence are already appearing. At the table the daughter is sometimes high-spirited and childlike and then again withdrawn and moody. 'Never mind,' she says when the father asks what's wrong.

Right after dinner she goes upstairs. Doors and hallways can't muffle the clear sound of the flute. She plays a sad dance, a siciliano, in perfect rhythm, in a solemn tempo. The father and the mother look at each other, smiling.

Variation 8

'I simply can't. I don't want to either. I don't want it to *be* like that!'

'And what exactly do you mean?' asks the therapist.

The girl sighs and sniffs. She grabs a Kleenex from the box that stands next to her. She wipes her eyes and sits up straight.

'The responsibilities. All that you have to do when you're an adult. Manage money. Keep track of things. Make plans. When I do one thing, I neglect the other. Make dates with friends. Remember birthdays. Go to my parents'. Sometimes I do it all, and then, after a week, there's another stack of bills again. It never stops!'

'It's too much for you?'

The girl nods. 'I want it to be *done*. But it's never done. It's part of life. Shit!'

'Whose fault is that? It sounds like a reproach,' the therapist says carefully.

The girl explodes in anger; her eyes darken and with both hands, she grips the arms of the chair.

Variation 8

'She never told me, Mum. She acted as if everything was fun. As if everything would work out, that life would then be normal, like before, happy, without problems. She never said that it wouldn't be fun at all, that the crap doesn't quit, that you have to be constantly busy with duties and commitments. She didn't prepare me for that. She acted as if life was a party. That's not true.'

'Maybe she thought it was wonderful, with you.'

Silence. Crying. Blowing her nose.

'I told her, not too long ago. That she had lied to me. That upset her. I felt sorry for her.'

'You have the wrong impression of things,' says the therapist. 'It is more difficult than you thought. Perhaps you want to do it too well?'

'But it *has* to be done well,' says the girl. 'She herself does things very well. Mum, I mean. She went and helped me again after that conversation. Together to the bank to top up my account. But that doesn't help—next month it will be chaotic again. How can I learn—study, I mean—if I'm busy with my life all day long?'

'Have you ever thought about the fact that you don't have to see all your friends every week? If you change it to once a month, you'll have lot more time left.'

The girl shook her head. 'I have to be a good friend, someone who is always available and has time. But I *have* no time. And I can't say 'no' when someone calls.' She bursts out laughing. 'Hopeless!'

The therapist shifts in her seat. 'You are angry at your mother because she has misinformed you. You can't do anything about that. But you demand a lot from yourself, and that's something that you *can* change. You can start with your schedule.'

'What should I say then?'

'You could say: it's inconvenient right now; can we make a date in two weeks? For instance.'

'It's like waves,' says the girl as she pulls her organiser from her purse. 'They come at you, unstoppable, and sometimes there's a really high one in between. You can't escape them, and it will always be like that. I have to get used to it. To the money as well. I have more money than my girlfriends but mine is always gone. And then comes another wave of misery. I can't sleep because of it, and yet I *have* to sleep.'

'What do you do then?'

'Smoke pot. Or I drink some wine. That's not good either—I know!'

'Do you ever sleep well?'

The girl slumps in the chair and laughs through her tears: 'When I sleep at my parents'. At home. I'm twenty-two!'

As she goes to leave she stands in the middle of the room to put on her vest, then a jumper, over it her coat, and then a shawl. She collects her purse and plastic bags and then places everything back on the floor to shake the therapist's hand.

'Thanks! See you next week.'

∞

Four times an ornamented ascending triad and four times a descending one, with the right hand. Then the same pattern with the left hand. It resembled an etude, the waves of sixteenth notes that followed each other relentlessly. After the double bar in the second part, it began to get out of control until, somewhere halfway down the page, things stalled in a mournful lament. After that the misery started again. A vigorous end with a dry, cascading run. Tricky to split up between two hands. It needed cutting and pasting to assign the voices to the most suitable hand.

The tragic turn in the middle of the second part, measures 23 and 24 to be exact, was present in most of the variations. And in the aria itself, and there perhaps at its most desperate. In a forward-rattling, fast and seemingly light-hearted Variation, it was particularly noticeable, thought the woman. As if Bach put a marginal comment at the physical pleasure of playing, as if he even called indirect attention to the underlying essence of his work. Or did she make that up? The composer had been silent for hundreds of years. Perhaps he had even delighted in the cheerful, challenging passages of this complicated work. Perhaps she interpreted what she had read quite wrongly and put something into it that didn't belong there at all.

Yet she could not hear it differently. Hidden under the torrent of well-ordered strands of notes something, someone, asked a plaintive question and was immediately drowned out by the resumed athleticism of the opening. But the lament stayed with you.

The Variations lay like shiny pearls on a strand for everyone to see. For centuries people have been swooning in admiration at the ingenious construction of this work. Anyone who studied it became impressed by the breadth of its expressive possibilities, its swift changes of character, its technical mastery.

It could be, thought the woman, that this one-and-a-half measure filled with despair was the most brilliant invention of the whole cycle. Bach showed that a dangerous black hole lay hidden under the flawless, glorious surface, a hole that you could punch through just like that. Your fingers would encounter a void.

Variation 9, canon at the third

She felt that the third canon, which was answered at the third, was too perfect a song, almost haughtily serene. It made her furious, and while learning the notes she played it on purpose in a sing-song and pedantic manner. Why can't I enjoy it, she thought, why do I torture myself with such senseless rebelliousness and distrust the foolish remarks that Bach himself made about his music?

The purpose of music is to imitate nature, he believed. No, not the mountains, brooks and trees, but human nature. Inner life. Our state of mind. As a boy, Bach had been overwhelmed by the music that his great uncle Johann Christoph (the "sensitive" Bach) composed.

The woman could imagine this, since once, in her car, she had been overcome by an exceptional song of lamentation written by Johann Christoph: an alto voice accompanied by nothing but low strings and embellished by one single violin. "Oh that my head were waters, and mine eyes a fountain of tears, that I might weep day and night, day and night." She had stopped the car alongside the road, had turned up the volume of the radio, had listened breathlessly. Unfortunately, the piece lasted only seven minutes at most. Later, in her urge for documentation, she had of course searched high and low for a score which, when she finally found it, could only confirm what she had heard. Day high, night low, descending triplets like rolling tears: the music sketched the emotions with almost laughable accuracy. Except that it was far from laughable; it choked your throat with misery.

In the canon she was working on there was nothing that recalled fits of weeping or of self-pity. On the contrary, the melody was steady, the rhythm tranquil, the musical exposition controlled. She was struck by the notion of a false simplicity; the harmonies were more complicated than you would think at a first hearing and seemed to announce all kinds of fury and calamity under the gentle surface. Or was that a projection of her own feelings?

A twelve-year-old girl, thought the mother, a model of flawlessness right before the start of puberty. She can dance and skate; she can read text and music. She knows every day which clothes she wants to wear. She oversees her world. Sometimes she suspects that her vision will become clouded, but not now, not yet. That was the third canon.

∞

'But you know no one who goes to that school,' says the mother. 'Wouldn't you rather go with your girlfriends?'

'Aren't I allowed to choose? I'm choosing this one. I'm sure. It's really quite good. And it's near your work! We can get together at lunchtime—then we'll go and have a treat together.'

They are sitting in the garden; it is early spring. No wind, mild weather. Buds swelling on the branches of the apple tree.

The sun places the daughter's face in bright light. The way she sits on that garden chair, thinks the mother, with that straight back, wearing a pink T-shirt, looking as if she has to reassure me. Invulnerable and fragile at the same time.

The past weeks were dominated by choosing a school. The parents visited five schools with the daughter, all of which had a good reputation. five assembly halls or gymnasiums, five speeches from principals, five mornings among alarmingly tall and noisy children. The daughter did not choose the school that focused on music. Not the high school where the city's elite sent their children, and not the welcoming high school with the giant beech tree in the courtyard. To the mother's dismay, the daughter chose the small, stuffy school, the only one that had "Christian" in its name. The mother supports the separation of church and state. And education. The mother does not appreciate religious teachers.

As she looks at the daughter's resolute face, she tries, in spite of her prejudices, to see the positive sides of the decision. Bible stories, so that the great paintings become comprehensible. Serious teachers with an overdeveloped conscience. Order, regularity, exactness. Revolting. I should not set her against it; I must support her. She wants this. That is what the mother thinks.

The father takes the girl on the first day of school. With her new backpack on her lap she sits in the front seat of the car in her recently purchased, slightly too large blue coat. The mother takes the small face between her hands, kisses her brave child and waves at the car.

'Just stop at the corner,' says the daughter. 'I'll walk the rest of the way.'

'Are you sure you know how to get back? Where the bus stop is? Do you have your pass? Shall I come and pick you up anyway?'

She sighs. 'No, Dad. We've practised. I'm going by bus.'

He strokes the short hair. She gets out and heaves the backpack around her shoulders. Then she walks to the new school where she knows no one, where everything is different from what she is used to, where everyone is bigger, older, more experienced than she.

'I already have two girlfriends—they live this way as well. We went on the bus together. Tomorrow morning, too. During recess we'll go to De Kombuis—that's a kind of cafeteria in the basement. The older kids stand outside. They smoke! We sat down at a table to eat.'

'But how …?' asks the mother.

'Simple. Ask: What's your name. I sat next to a girl with an organiser like mine. We're getting extra drawing because the religion teacher is very sick and won't come back for a while. Now I have to go upstairs to pack my bag for tomorrow. I don't want bananas anymore, they get all gooey.'

The mother sees with pride and amazement how the child settles in at the new school within a few weeks, how she develops opinions about the rules and about the teachers, how she determines distance and closeness with new friends. By the time the last leaves fall off the trees, the daughter has become an experienced fresher.

∞

For a whole hour the woman had worked on the canon. She had delineated the upper voice solidly and made sure that the second voice, a third lower, a measure later, a fraction softer, followed timidly. Although the voices were in harmony with each other, they never really coincided; the second one remained a rather worried commentary on the first one. The underlying bass line made its presence felt, especially toward the end, pushed things forward, and concluded resolutely. The woman did her best with the imitations that she coloured with subtle dynamic differences.

What had Bach written on the title page of the Goldberg Variations? His music served to "transform the heart." She had to grant that, because the immersion in the canon had wiped away her annoyance. Anger had been replaced by a sense of detachment, the excited heartbeat had adapted to the steady tempo. The heart had calmed down.

Variation 10, fughetta

Four has become a pleasing number since the family consists of four members. Rather the wind directions and the seasons than the Three Kings and the Trinity, thinks the mother. She can pull one child onto each hip and run away, if she has to. The family is exactly the right size: four chairs at the table; four seats in the car; two and two on the bicycle. When she asks the children what they think about having another baby, they scream in horror. Unthinkable.

    The parents' friends also have two children. The combination of the families gives joy to all of them. Christmas holidays in a rented farmhouse. Amazing how the children adapt, thinks the mother. Her son is in the same grade as their friends' older boy. Their younger child, also a boy, is still small. The daughter leads the foursome but also knows how to conform to the boys' wishes. She plays soccer with them, tripping awkwardly over clumps of grass; she and the older boy play opposite her brother who has the youngest one on his side. In this way the teams are equally strong. The combinations shift as in a dance; at the table she sits next to her brother. During games she takes care of the youngest boy and battles with him against the two others.

In the summer both families drive one behind the other to France, in cars with enormous camping tents, chairs, and tables lashed on top. At the end of a wide valley between snow-covered mountains—alternately cursing and screaming with laughter—they set up tents, fold out awnings, set out tables and eight chairs, and play housekeeping. The *Amsterdams Dagblad* and *La Dépêche du Midi*, lukewarm beer, Fanta, and wine. The mother and the daughter make cocktail appetisers which they serve, nicely arranged, on tennis rackets covered with aluminum foil. Fellow campers are observed and provided with histories and names. The four children go off to inspect the swimming pool. The daughter leads, in her blue bathing suit. She has tied a towel around her waist. The boys, carrying flippers and soccer balls, follow her. The swimming pool shimmers in the distance.

At dinner the father asks if they have made any friends yet. The two older boys shake their heads. 'They speak French! They think we're odd. They don't understand us.'

"They're looking, though,' says the youngest. 'The one with the lock of hair in front of his eyes was lying there and watching us the whole time, and then he'd go and whisper with his friends. Did you see that too?'

The girl nods.

'They're looking at *you*! You're our secret weapon! You have to entice them, and then we'll have friends. If it works. Then you catch one, and I'll jump forward: I'm her brother! *Bonsoir*!'

They are doubled up with laughter over their plates of frites.

It gets dark. The four of them leave for the square at the entrance of the campground. There you can play ping pong and drink coca-cola at marble tables. That's where the young people gather. The boys have put on Ajax and Barcelona shirts, the daughter, a skirt. 'We're going contact hunting!' she says, smiling.

After an hour the parents can no longer contain themselves. Time for an evening walk to the village. They take the back exit in order to stay at a distance from the young people's area. On the way back, they walk straight through it and stop at the table where their children are playing cards, all talking at the same time, first looking at the faces of their parents, then again at the playing cards in their hands.

'I said you should get on the table. Dance! Striptease!'

The daughter laughs. 'We should make a song and then perform it here. That will make them listen.'

'Soccer,' says the older boy earnestly. 'That interests everybody. Organise a tournament. They're just standing there, messing around at the ping pong tables. They're not even playing.'

'But *we* are doing something,' says the daughter. 'Playing hearts. I have an idea: if they see that we're having fun, they'll come and look and we'll make contact. We'll just grab them.' She shuffles the cards—she always has a deck of playing cards with her—she lets them form into two stacks with coordinated movements of her thumbs, and deals.

The smallest boy is quiet. He looks at the girl and receives his playing cards almost gratefully. '*Merci*,' he whispers. 'We have to speak French, as a start. *Tu es mon amie.*'

The parents walk back to the tents. The children's voices—high, low, mixed with exclamations and giggling, muttering, chattering—fade away and dissolve in the evening sounds. The father opens a bottle. The waiting begins.

∞

The tenth variation was a small fugue for four voices. Not a real one, thought the woman, because the fugue theme had no fixed counter melody and not much happened with the theme, no inversion, no crab motion, or metric contraction or extension. The thirty-two measures did not offer enough space for such feats. Four voices in different positions, that sang the same melody one after the other. Never at the same time, as if they listened respectfully to each other. A cheerful conversation.

In the past she had found fugues difficult. Too cerebral, too carefully thought out. So much fuss with the fingering, to play all the parts nicely legato. Embarrassing when, after weeks of practising, you suddenly encountered an inversion of the theme you had never noticed. So difficult to execute complicated ornaments in excruciating positions, with the little finger and fourth finger, while the rest of the hand played a melody or held a chord.

Now the fugue is my salvation, she thought. No form requires your attention so completely and appeals so little to immediate feelings. A fugue is seldom moving or beautiful. A fugue is a structure that has to be painstakingly put together, layer on layer, with no errors in construction.

She worked on the web of voices. She made sure that every entry was clearly audible, even when it was a middle voice. Everyone had a turn in this friendly conversation. The lowest voice started and sang two measures alone. It was the only voice that held forth for the entire fugue and lent contrast to, needled or supported the other voices. The voice that carried the piece.

Variation 11

There are things that you dread, not because they are extremely difficult but because they seem strange to you, thought the woman. Variation 11 was such a "thing." The strangest thing was the playing technique because what had to be played was not so odd. Descending scales in 3/4 time, after four bars transformed into exuberant ascending triads. Those have to be played with the wrong hand in a contorted position. Would it help if she had a harpsichord with two manuals? If she sat as low as Glenn Gould? If she took out the lid behind the keyboard?

It was basically an athletic challenge. The woman didn't like sport. The woman was no good at it and had always felt awkward and slightly embarrassed whenever she played.

Sport had entered her life through her son who, when he wasn't even two years old, could already imitate perfectly the shot-putters on television, including the helplessly spinning skip after the throw. From the time he was four years old, he had longed for a soccer ball, with a passion that the woman recognised from her own love of music. The local soccer club set the minimum age for membership at six; the son spent the long years until he was admitted to the youngest group in intense expectation. Before the summer holidays, the woman drove him to Joro Sporting Goods to buy the uniform. White shorts with red piping. Small soccer boots, Puma brand, stitched up by Johan Cruijff himself.

The boy was not afraid at all on the field. He had fun. The children got in each other's way on the scaled-down soccer field, just like the fingers of both hands in Variation 11. The hunger for the ball, for the kicking, drove them together into the penalty area. There were no tactics; there was only the desire to touch the ball. The woman had watched it with admiration, every Saturday. The daughter stood next to her. Afterwards they ate croquettes in the stinking canteen where the son seemed to feel at home as much as in a living room. The croquette seller had only one tooth, and, according to the boy, slept under the counter at night. He told this with a certain longing in his voice. Why would you go out into the world when you could live next to a soccer field?

Perhaps the woman should learn something from her child's behaviour during his pre-school years. Not to worry about technique, only fervently desire the key, *that* one *there*, down below, and then the next one. Then the movements of the arms would adjust automatically to the playing fingers, in a completely natural way that soared above tactical considerations. No body, no shoulders. Only fingertips.

∞

'I want to do rowing,' she says. She grasps her cutlery, makes a fist and moves the handles as if she is arduously pulling oars through water. The mother gets out of the way of the fork.

Variation 11

'It's really fantastic. You have to train, and when you can do it a little, you have to row in competitions. They have parties in the clubhouse. There's a bar with a terrace.'

That is where the mother sits on a Saturday, like a sailor's wife, on the lookout for her daughter. On the wide river there are incredibly long boats with at least eight rowers in them, solitary singles, and out-of-place pleasure boats. Coaches with large megaphones ride on the cycle path and scream commands to their pupils. On the other side lies a cemetery with its own landing.

The daughter rows in a coxless pair with a friendly boy of sixteen or so. 'He is so sweet, actually too sweet. We talk about everything, you can do that with him.' When the two of them carried the boat from the boathouse to the water, the mother had looked carefully at the boy. Why can't she fall in love with him, she had thought, such an obviously nice person who understands her and with whom she can laugh? Why does she always choose difficult friends with dark hair and dark souls?

The daughter's back, in a blue-white club suit, comes into view. Both rowers pull their oars energetically through the water, in a pleasant rhythm but with great force. The boat starts to deviate from its course in the middle of the river. They don't see where they are going, thinks the mother. They want to arrive as fast as possible but don't know where. No time to look over their shoulders, no interest. No mistrust.

The skeg of the boat gets into the reeds that grow abundantly alongside the bank of the river. The boat loses speed, is stuck, and slowly turns sideways in the current. The coach, a heavy youth on an old bicycle, arrives panting, gets off the bike and starts railing at them. The rowers are helpless with laughter. Howling with laughter, the daughter is doubled up over the oars and grabs her friend's arm with her wet hands.

'Stupid!' yells the coach. 'You have to look out of the corner of your eyes. Pay attention! This always happens to you. Bunch of amateurs!'

Wet and tired, they join the mother on the terrace, still laughing.

'I said to that loudmouth: "What's your problem? We're having fun. Calm down." He can't. We went fast, didn't we?'

The partner, who has a pleasant face, nods. 'That river just runs the wrong way. If they shift it, we'll be first. That's how fast we go.'

'I think I close my eyes,' says the daughter. 'I feel the speed, the water. I don't think when I row. I don't care where we go.'

∞

If she didn't approach this properly right away, she would continue to face number 11 reluctantly, thought the woman. That way it would never amount to anything. She could not, as she used to, blithely throw her arms onto the keyboard, let her fingers follow the melody lines, and just see where the ship would run aground.

With the help of Kirkpatrick's score, she shifted the voices. She played the high notes with the right hand, the low notes with the left hand, regardless of the melodic line. Striving for the most economical movement seemed to her both a professional and a physical activity. As long as she kept following the musical lines in her head and took care that her fingers reproduced these lines with a slight emphasis, nothing could happen. Then she would know where she was going.

Like a tranquil river, the music played between the banks, the waves rippled, sometimes splashed, pushed along everything that floated on the water; the woman did not surrender to pleasure or to confidence but kept her muscles under control and paid attention with all her mind.

Variation 12, canon at the fourth

When does puberty come, thinks the mother. When is she really going to talk back and be rebellious?

Now. The daughter quarrels with the father. Slamming doors. Footsteps stomping on the stairs. Shouting.

The door of the girl's room is locked. The mother stands in front of it, in the hallway, and talks to photos and posters. The argument is about nothing. Shoes lying in the middle of the room, a coat flung down—the usual irritations caused by a child growing up. The parents function as a punching bag, as a sounding board for the fury of the child at the world's inflexibility. Soon she'll come downstairs, in time for dinner.

The mother lowers herself by crouching down and leans with her back against the wall. The feeble smell of a cigarette seeps through the crack of the door. The mother smiles. For some months there have been fewer cigarettes in the house than she thought. So this is where they are.

The rebelliousness of the daughter is a challenge to harmony. The mother is a heavy smoker; she reaches for her cigarettes in the pockets of her cardigan. Smoking together, on both sides of the door.

The same. Different. It bothers the mother that the daughter prefers mathematics to Latin at school. Greek is totally out of the question. How can you grow up without Tacitus, without Homer?

'The teacher is so stupid! There's nothing to it at all. You can still change subjects at Christmas. I'm going to stop it. What's the use anyway?'

'When you've studied classical languages you can understand all the difficult words. All the medical terms.'

The daughter snorts scornfully.

'I don't have to like what *you* think is important. That *is* possible, you know. It doesn't matter. It's simply like that, Mum.'

Yes, it's simply like that. When the daughter looks for a holiday job, she doesn't become a nurse's aide in the hospital. The smell in the dishwashing kitchen, thinks the mother, that peculiar and sad smell of urine and Lysol. The sound of your quick steps in the deserted hallway at night. The daughter is insensitive to these things. She is going to serve in an Italian restaurant. Dressed in a short, black skirt she whirls, dancing past the tables. At the end of the evening she sings a duet with a waiter. She receives paper currency as tips.

The maths teacher is crazy about her and makes her feel she can do everything. She does equations that the mother has never been able to understand. For working them out neatly, she uses a Snoopy ruler. Logarithms and cosines have no secrets for her.

The daughter can become angry—she shows it very clearly now. She is able to say no to things that don't please her. Without thinking.

She can have secrets; she can conceal things. It is difficult for her, but she can. She calls from a telephone booth in the city to say that she is safe and staying at a friend's; they're almost ready for bed; it was nice, but they're tired now. Then she goes back into the disco.

The mother admires the way the child handles distance and closeness, how with small acts she safeguards her freedom within the mother-daughter relationship.

The door of the room opens. Smoke drifts into the hall.

'What's for dinner? I'm hungry.'

'Just open the window,' says the mother. 'Air it out a little. Right?' With her hand she strokes the daughter's soft hair. The child allows it and smiles.

∞

The fourth was an unpleasant interval, thought the woman. Irritating and loud. The ascending fourth called for an action which you weren't in the mood for. An almost military atmosphere of duty hung around that interval. Marching songs. The national anthem, the *Wilhelmus*. If you heard both notes, not one after the other but at the same time, it created a mockingly empty feeling. Emptiness wasn't bad. An octave produced a calm, simple emptiness. The emptiness of the fifth held a promise and was soft, vulnerable. The emptiness of the fourth was difficult to bear. The other intervals were not empty. The second and the seventh were fleeting harmonies, searching for a resolution. You could hear the third and sixth as sweet, harmonic, complete.

What drivel, thought the woman, and concentrated on the canon at the fourth. She turned away from the window behind the grand piano, the enormous window that had a view of the world. On the other side of it postmen and deliverymen walked back and forth, people looking for doorbells and conversations. Bushes grew there, and trees that produced fruit and then dropped their leaves. Birds screeched. Time passed.

The canon stood on the rack. The bass with its unrelentingly hammering recurring notes was the foundation above which the two voices spoke to each other. They interrupted each other. They contradicted each other. Whatever one said was repeated exactly the other way around by the other. In the first part it was the upper voice that carried the theme; after the double bar the lower voice, that contradicting voice. It started first, and then the other one joined later—in the inversion, still with one fourth difference—and gradually both voices created a profound change of mood. They adjusted audibly to each other; they repeated sad passages after each other and together came to a plaintive ending: a descending tonic triad. The bass continued to simmer a little and struggled upward in a seventh. It no longer mattered; it was actually superfluous.

Outside the window, twilight had set in. One by one the streetlights turned on, first hesitantly, with flickering light, then calmly and assuredly. The woman sat in the circle of light radiated by the piano lamp and worked tirelessly at the last notes. She wouldn't give in; she continued undeterred and doggedly until her fingers had adjusted to the fanciful line of the voices and until she had point and counterpoint in her fingers as a matter of course.

Variation 13

There was the grand piano, and there was the table. The woman went back and forth between the two places, driven more by aversion than desire. The thirteenth variation: the first one that had a genuinely slow tempo, a sad sarabande surrounded by endless garlands of tender notes. Of course it was in a major key but all the same inexpressibly disconsolate, driving her to the table. She took up her pencil. Recounting episodes from the life of a child was the least you could expect from a mother. Based on the mother's memories or on her imagination. Starting chronologically, from photo albums, or from something else that swept the ideas to the surface. Music.

The problem with the table was that there was no keyboard on it, and no music rack. This tempted her to stare outside. The woman looked. She saw autumnal fields with ditches between them. A flock of black birds circled above the meadow and finally landed in a mud puddle. To be a bird like that, thought the woman, one of the birds from that flock, to do what you must do, what the bird in front of you did—ascend, land, peck in the mud. Towards evening, alight in a tree, among the other birds, as part of the flock. Would she then wonder whether she was sitting too close, or whether the place that she took on the black branch was the right one? Perhaps it was difficult to be part of a flock. The woman thought of the plumes of steam that in cities like New York or Washington worked their way, hissing, through dollar-sized openings in iron lids in the middle of the road. The wind dragged the white cloud against the asphalt, cars drove through it with their heavy tyres, but the plume of smoke rose again and again, blowing and whistling, with unrelenting strength. Where did that steam come from, what happened under that surface, and why did everyone act as if nothing was wrong? Sad to identify with a cloud of steam, thought the woman. Nothing was more tenuous, weaker, and more meaningless.

Back at the piano she placed her right hand in her lap and with her left hand played the double bass line. The theme with the little finger, the compelling tenor part above it. Slowly, slowly. With utmost concentration she imagined the whimsical line of the descant above that duet. With her innermost ear she heard very clearly how the soprano wavered, ascended with delight, fell back down almost disappointed and then, started once again, a restless but steady rise. Toward the end the song soared, hissing and spurting, and rose above everything, like a pale, expanding cloud, unexpectedly bowing its head in the last measure. She lifted her right hand and began to play.

∞

"Oto-rhino-laryngology" it says in big letters on the sign above the entrance of the outpatient clinic. If she had learned

Variation 13

Greek, the daughter who stands very close to her would know where she was. The mother leans against the counter and opens her mouth as soon as the receptionist looks up. No, don't do it, it's *her* doctor's visit. She is twenty-four.

'I have an appointment at phoniatrics,' says the daughter. It sounds resolute and confident, but the mother hears the voice as flat and high. Nerves.

They are sent to a waiting area where a man sits with cotton balls in his nose. A crying child keeps bringing its hands to its ears; an old lady spits furtively into a small cup. Mother and daughter both pick up a magazine and tell each other bits of information they read about. They have plenty of time. The daughter crosses her legs in knee-high boots and digs in her purse for chapstick. She has pulled her hair back tightly into a ponytail.

'Mum, why am I doing this?'

The fluorescent light high against the ceiling flickers on and off uncertainly. She does this because she wants something, because she has a passion. 'I'll finish my studies, really,' she had said, 'you don't need to worry. And then I'll teach, two days a week or so, at my old school. I'm sure that's possible. What I want to do more than anything is to sing. Become a singer. Study at the conservatory.'

The mother had nodded, acknowledging. Of course, if there was anyone who had a talent for singing, a natural feeling for music, it was the daughter. 'You just think so because you're my mother—that doesn't help me!' But the singing teacher thought so too; that's why they were here in the outpatient clinic, waiting for the doctor who specialised in phoniatrics. Anyone who aspired to a singing career had to undergo an examination; proficiency and talent were not enough. Throat, larynx, and vocal cords—the instrument concealed in the slender neck of the daughter had to receive a certificate of soundness.

A thin woman with short grey hair invites them into a large room. She says that she examines all the candidates for the entrance exam, nothing to worry about. Has she noticed the tension on the daughter's face? No, she is filling in a form and doesn't look up for quite a while. The mother pushes her chair back a bit and listens. The daughter reports—how much she practises, that in addition to vocalising and arias, she also sings with a band, that she is sometimes hoarse but often not at all, that she…The daughter's back is perfectly straight. She answers all the questions honestly and confidently, as if she is convinced that everyone will cooperate in order to realise her dream. The mother takes shallow breaths.

'We'll take a look,' says the doctor.

Scales, high and low, whispering and singing at the top of her voice; growling, sighing, moaning. The daughter produces the requested sounds and meanwhile the doctor looks in her throat, squeezes her instrument past the perfect teeth and feels the neck. 'Atypical dysphonia,' the mother hears her mumble. The form on the table becomes filled with pluses, minuses, illegible scribbles.

'I want to look at your vocal cords. I'll place a camera in your throat, and then we can see *here* what happens *there* when you sing.' She points at a large television screen and pushes a large object into the daughter's throat. 'Singing is the most beautiful thing in the world,' the daughter had said. 'When I sing, everything is fine. I want it.'

The daughter doesn't gag but follows all the orders dutifully. The screen shows shiny, pink structures that move when the daughter makes a sound, two fleshy walls with a mysterious, dark slit between them. They move toward each other and then draw back. 'Once again,' says the doctor, 'I want to look at it carefully one more time.'

Then they are back at the table. 'A defective closure,' says the doctor. 'There are a few nodules on the vocal cords.

Variation 13

Most likely you've been singing too much, and incorrectly, with that band. You can get rid of them with exercise; that's not serious. But the anatomy of your vocal cords is not ideal. Incomplete closure of the vocal folds. It's a predisposition. Just as one person has long legs and the other has short ones. Nothing can be done about it. It makes your voice unreliable. Therefore unsuited for the profession. If you do plenty of speech therapy you can, of course, continue singing. As an amateur.'

The mother freezes as though she has received news of a death. The daughter will never sing as Susanna, with her big aria in the second act of *Figaro*; never as Zerlina, as the soloist in the Brahms Requiem, in Bach cantatas. The mother is indignant and crushed at the same time. Then she gets up and walks out behind the daughter who, head held high and stony-faced, leaves the room without saying another word to the doctor. In the parking lot the daughter kicks the tyres of the car as hard as she can. 'As if a cow like her knows anything about it; I'll go to someone else; I don't have to take this from a witch like that. I'll show her that it's all wrong. Defective closure! That woman is defective herself.'

Her chin trembles. Dejected, they sit staring at the misted-up windshield. 'She had hairs on her chin,' says the daughter. 'I know of a good speech therapist, from my singing teacher.'

The speech therapist will give exercises. Animal sounds will fill the farmhouse where the family spends the Christmas holidays. The daughter retreats with disciplined regularity in order to do her rehabilitation exercises. The nodules on the delicate vocal cords will disappear. The singing technique will be completely rebuilt, from the bottom up. There is no more smoking and drinking. In the annual performance of the Mozart Requiem, the daughter will sing contralto instead of soprano in order not to put too much pressure on the voice.

For two years she will fight against the verdict, against disappointment, against her anatomy. This first real setback causes a wound. Going to the opera is unbearable. She is upset, moody, is sleepless. She is sad. She bursts out in anger when the mother sums up the remaining possibilities and urges her to take the oboe out of the cupboard again. It takes time. It's terrible.

Then she'll bow her head and acknowledge defeat. Time blows its healing breath that will slowly fuse into a scar.

Variation 14

'When I came to her high school,' says the daughter's girlfriend, 'that was the third year, and she was already the most popular girl in school. Or well on her way, at any rate. It was a tremendously nice class, and that was because of her. Always thinking up jokes, up for everything, having everyone join in. I wasn't used to that at all.'

The mother sits across from the friend in a café. They order coffee with a lot of milk.

'She was at her best at school parties. When she entered, you immediately felt: now it's starting. The programme simply couldn't do without her. Really amazing. She performed a difficult duet on the oboe with that strange teacher who played the violin, and after that she sang in the band of the art teacher, the one with the beard, you remember? She was on the stage the whole evening.'

The music is too loud; the mother and the girlfriend bend their heads closer together across the narrow table.

'I still remember really well how it was in the fifth year. A year before the final exit exam. She'd had all kinds of boyfriends, but now she was aiming for the most popular boy. And he for her. They had been eyeing each other for weeks. And then, during an afternoon recess—I was standing upstairs near that big staircase—she suddenly appeared at the end of the hall with a big smile; she was wearing that red dress. She raised her arms in the air and shouted: 'We kissed!' As if she had won the thousand metres. I really had to laugh!'

The mother takes a cigarette. She listens.

'The final party was a few days later. Actually it was a soap opera, and all of us were caught up in it. I thought it was a difficult period, most of us did, I think. Fights with your parents, uncertainty about what to do after school's over, shit with boyfriends. Pimples, divorces, eating disorders. Everyone had problems. She didn't, then. It was her world, and she felt at home, completely contented. I still see her standing on the stage during that party. She sang the closing song with a few others, some soul number. Very free, very intense. After that we were supposed to dance.

'I don't know if I remember correctly, but as far as I can recall no one would start, we all stood in a circle around the dance floor while the band was already playing. Then she stepped forward. She looked at the boy, the cutest, the most sought-after boy in the school, and he had to go into the circle. They couldn't keep their eyes off each other. They started to dance, ever closer together. We clapped and whistled; the music became more stirring, it looked like a well-planned theatre act but it was real, it simply happened. They moved toward each other; they touched each other, until everything ended in The Kiss. We screamed and stomped, of course. From that moment on it was really on.'

Variation 14

The mother stirred the lukewarm coffee. 'He was pleasant,' she said. 'We played games; he liked that. And they were nice to each other, certainly in the beginning.'

'Yes, later on it became difficult. He'd tell her how to pack her suitcase. Smug. It made her unsure, as if she didn't know anything or couldn't do anything. But in the beginning it was a movie, a fairy tale. An ideal romance that we all longed for. And she danced in that large circle and let us believe in it.'

The mother and the friend light cigarettes. They sit together quietly and watch how the smoke moves above the table.

∞

Such a cheerful piece in between two intensely sad variations: what should I do with that, thought the woman, as she lowered herself, sighing, onto the piano stool. Skip it. But that was not possible. Anyway, she was fed up with sighing and moaning, such posturing. Thirty-two measures in G major. Just practise, think about nothing else.

Something new started every four measures, and the trick was to connect these heterogeneous elements to each other in some way. Finding a tempo in which all the fragments came into their own didn't work. I'm involved with something that I can no longer feel, thought the woman. That restless youthfulness, that abrupt changing into another idiom, going along idly and finding everything equally beautiful—I can't do that. She took the metronome out of the cupboard. If you didn't understand something automatically, you could use tools. Passages that she judged too slow turned out to be too fast, and the reverse. Good. At least she knew that. Adjust. Again. It became a dazzling whole, around the mechanical metronome ticks. She drilled into her head the chords of the measures in which the hands tumbled over each other; a diminuendo in every measure but a slow crescendo over the four measures, and then even more in the measures that followed. Or would it be better to do a gradual diminuendo and end in a whisper?

She shouldn't get annoyed at her indecision. The nice thing about Bach was that there were no dynamic indications in the score; you could make all that up yourself. And you didn't have to set it down—it could be one way one time, and the next time another. Despite her hesitations, she entered the small universe to look around, amazed at the cheerfulness, surprised by the spontaneity, alert to all sudden turns.

Did it storm and rain outside? She wouldn't know. The tragedy of the preceding variation and the desolation of the next one had faded from her consciousness. For over an hour she was absorbed in the dance-like, bright enchantment of the two pages of the score that stood in front of her on the rack.

Variation 15, canon at the fifth

The first variation in a minor key, only now, at the halfway point of the whole structure. The woman stared at the notes and thought of the composer. Although she had read thick books about him, she knew very little. Facts without significant context: when he examined an organ; in what period the partitas were composed; that he moved from Köthen to Leipzig. That he was a deeply religious man. She couldn't imagine any of it very well and was sorry that she didn't know how the works had sounded or who had played them. The cantatas and the passions were for the Church—that was obvious. But the instrumental music that he seemed so proud of?

Who knows, perhaps the first cellist of the court orchestra came to Bach's house after dinner, panting under the weight of his instrument. They retreated into his study but left the door open. The musician placed the cello between his knees and let it rest on his solid calves because the pin for anchoring the cello in the floor had not yet been invented. He pulled the bow-shaped stick calmly across the strings and tuned. He wore a wig. The music, on loose pages, stood on the stand in the middle of the room. Bach himself was sitting at the composing table with a hand under his chin and waited.

'You've had these things at home for a week,' he said. 'Go ahead. I want to hear fireworks.'

But there were no fireworks. The man played the sarabande from the fifth cello suite, a simple song in C minor, without counter melodies, double stops or ornaments. When the first notes sounded, Bach looked up, surprised, and made a dismissive gesture with his free hand. 'Oh, just leave it, I want to transcribe that suite for the lute; why don't you choose something that I'm not really satisfied with?' His words ended in mumbling. After three measures he was silent.

The woman imagined how the music soared and increased in richness in the candle-lit room. How Anna Magdalena came and stood in the doorway. She didn't have to admonish the children at her skirt to be quiet but felt in the decreasing tension in their shoulders that they would continue to listen silently and intently. Perhaps it was then that she thought up the plan to copy out all the suites, on heavy paper, because that disorganised stack on the music stand was absolutely hopeless; it was a disgrace for such incredible music. The sarabande. A trifling melody, only a couple of notes. And yet the world ends. Did people cry in public during the first part of the eighteenth century? Anna Magdalena was moved to tears.

The woman considered it possible that Bach himself was slightly puffy-eyed when the cellist played his last note, that slowly fading high C. That he cleared his throat and asked for something faster, more virtuoso. The third suite, for example, with its imposing prelude. Had the essence of the sarabande disappeared when the house became filled with other notes? No, nothing ever disappeared for Bach. He retained the mood of the sarabande somewhere in his brilliant memory and evoked it again in this fifteenth Goldberg Variation. In small, chromatic steps he sketched pure sorrow, sung by three voices in a slow tempo.

The woman searched patiently for the correct fingering in order to perform everything beautifully legato and to use the weight of the hand to introduce subtle accents. Simple. It had to remain simple and transparent because what was set down in the notes was already tragic enough. Halfway in the second part of the piece there was a measure in which the upper voice was silent. The bass and the lower voice moved downward in an intangible idiom, for a moment detached from any key whatsoever, as if referring to music that would not be created until centuries later. The woman shivered. No sensitivity now, she thought, no stinging eyes or lump in the throat. Nonsense. The canon had to be performed, slowly and perfectly, up to and including the very last measure, in which the upper voice climbed higher and higher and the bass remained lying in the depth, as if he could not save the soprano and had to watch helplessly at how she took off and disappeared in the emptiest fifth that had ever sounded.

∞

The noise of a bicycle being flung against the outside wall. The mother notices and jumps up. The daughter must not have been able to stand it again in her room in the city where she has been living for a few months. About three times a week she arrives on her bicycle or asks to be picked up to come home to eat, study, and sleep. And then she leaves again with packets of coffee and toilet paper in her bag.

The front door is pushed open. Footsteps drum on the stairs and the girl disappears into her old room. The mother has gone to the stove to make tea, but she turns off the gas when she hears from upstairs the uncontrolled howls of a crying fit.

The child has pulled on worn jogging pants and the father's discarded jumper. She sits on the bed with her head on her knees. 'It's finished. He wants to be free. I restrict him!' Snot sticks to her upper lip. The mother gets a handkerchief and sits down next to the daughter. She holds her tightly and cleans her face. 'What a prick.'

'No!' counters the daughter, infuriated. 'He's not a prick. I love him. But I just don't know what he wants.'

The mother feels like crying with her. The daughter puts her head in her mother's lap and lets herself be embraced.

'It's so different from what I thought, Mum.' She sighs, a deep childlike sigh without any theatrics. 'Everything is already so difficult in the house, all that I have to manage. Eating, doing dishes, caring for the cat. And then this.' The mother strokes the daughter's hair. 'He says that he does love me, but he wants to be independent. I don't know how that works. I mean, why doesn't he explain how that goes?'

The mother bites her lip. She has no wise lessons to impart. She is bewildered, intensely alarmed about how life is forcing its way into the daughter's awareness. The mother of one of her school friends suddenly had cancer and died. A boy from her graduating class crashed to his death on his motorbike against a tree. An aeroplane crashed nearby and destroyed an apartment building where former classmates of the daughter lived. The daughter spends a lot of time with her motherless girlfriend, talks with the friends of the boy who was killed, and goes on a memorial walk for the victims of the plane crash. She does it all, thinks the mother, but what is happening is too much, too threatening to really feel it. How can you even imagine that a doctor tells a woman she has five months to live, that a nurse comes out of the operating theatre and tells the parents that the surgeon was unable to save their son, that a giant aeroplane falls burning from the sky five hundred metres from your parents' home?

The mother thinks in platitudes. That you feel small and powerless. That in contrast to every joy there is an immense sorrow that you are unaware of, and that you can usually ignore. But it is there, in this brutal world. That you cannot protect your children from it. That she, the mother, cannot teach her child how she should handle it, how she can bear this powerlessness. She herself is unable to. Who can?

That is why she sits silently in the girl's dismantled room and lets the daughter lean against her. She sees the curve of the belly under the elastic of the pants; at least she is eating enough. The daughter's breathing becomes gradually calmer, but the child remains lying down, nothing changes. Always, thinks the mother, always continue leaning against each other like this, powerless and sad. Always.

Variation 16, overture

'They're coming, Mummy, I hear the dogs!'

The daughter points to the other side of the bay. The mother comes and stands next to her and peers at where she is pointing. Where the path leaves the dark coniferous forest, two figures appear that are gradually illuminated more clearly by the evening sun. The first one, a large man's figure, clasps an object against his shoulder. Right behind him is a woman who carries something in her arms. Two black and white dogs are running in small circles around their feet.

The table is set under the large linden tree. Behind the garden, high on the spit of land that extends far into the lake, stands the summer home, black and austere. Here the family has spent practically all its summers; here the girl and the boy have learned to swim, to pick berries and to speak Swedish. Now they are nineteen and sixteen years old, thinks the mother, and still they want to come here, with us. Earlier in the day she and the daughter dragged the soaked laundry to the lake, past the anthill where they had once placed a dead viper and where they found the gnawed clean skeleton the next day; past the tall, blooming blue campanulas, and between the thick carpet of lingonberry bushes, to the open water that is so clear you can look down into a depth of a metre and a half. The daughter hadn't felt like doing it but had gone along anyway, sighing.

They had squatted down on the grey rock to slowly rinse the coiled up shirts and underpants, to wring them out, to sweep them though the water again, to wave them wildly through the air so that the water drops made stripes on the stone. In the next inlet they had seen a pike glide quickly into the reeds. Between rinsing and wringing they had smoked a cigarette, laughing at their clumsy, wet fingers. A new phase has started, the mother had thought, it has already started. She has taken her final exit exam, she will be a student, she will leave. Squeezing hard with both hands, she swept the daughter's blouse through the water again and again, as if she wanted to defer the act of placing it on the stack of finished laundry.

When the work was done, they took off their clothes to go into the lake. The water tasted metallic. She took the shampoo bottle from the ridge in the large rock and gave it to her daughter. With towers of foam on their heads they swam slowly into the open. The daughter glanced quickly at the reeds. Then, with noses squeezed shut, they lowered themselves underneath the surface, felt how their hair flared out in the water, and surfaced spluttering and laughing. Now the laundry hung on the lines behind the house.

The couple with the dogs comes closer on the path, along the bay that is fringed with juniper bushes.

'He has a violin!' the boy mutters. 'I thought that he would bring along that cow's horn.'

Before they left their house, the white house on the mountain, about two-thirds of a mile away from the black one, the neighbour had blown a signal which the boy had answered. At the entrance of the garden, the family waits for their neighbours. The neighbour smiles, lifts the basket with food that she carries in her arms and admonishes the jumping dogs. Her husband plays a folk song on his violin—a polka, thinks the woman, a 3/4 time that you can walk to while rocking gently. The instrument seems small and vulnerable in his strong hands. Suspenders stretch across his paunch, and on his head he wears a handkerchief with four knots like a cap. His red hair sticks out on all sides.

'I'll get the wine right now,' says the daughter. But by then the neighbours are there and everyone is kissing and laughing as if they haven't seen one another in ages; although it was only yesterday that they all brought in the hay, the son proudly driving around on the tractor and the daughter high on the cart to catch the compact bales.

The sun goes down and throws orange pools of light on the water. Yet it will remain light all night long—if you wish, you can still read a book in the garden at midnight. People pull up benches and wooden chairs. The daughter pours the wine; the neighbour unpacks her basket. The dogs lie obediently at the neighbour's feet, their heads with watchful eyes pressed close to the ground, their rumps taut as if they could just fly off as soon as they hear a command. The neighbour wipes the sweat from his face and gently taps the dogs' necks. Tomorrow the animals have to be in top shape because he is going to put them in the sheepdog competition. They will have to do what he says, even if it goes against their instinct; they should not run off but instead surround the small demonstration herd; they will herd the sheep into ever diminishing circles and chase them into the fold.

'Can we come along?' asks the boy. 'I'd like to see that.'

The neighbour, the man with the sheep, nods and smiles. The daughter pulls the napkins from the serving dishes. 'We picked blueberries, that will be dessert. There were so many mosquitoes!'

Then they sit silently together under the giant linden tree. From the crown of the tree they hear the vague humming of bees that are fooled by the light, that think it is still day, time to collect honey. The father points to the wall of stacked stones at the edge of the garden. On the top layer of stones lies an elongated, dark shape. They look. It's a hare; he rests stretched out on the warm rocks, not bothered by the six people under the linden tree.

'What a quiet evening,' the neighbour says softly. 'Soon the black-throated diver will call across the lake. A quiet evening.'

∞

Now I'm halfway, thought the woman at the piano. What possessed Bach to compose an overture in the middle of his Goldberg Variations? Barely recovered from the tranquil, sorrowful ending of the previous piece, you have to prepare for a full chord that sets in motion a stream of fanciful inventions. A new beginning? It seemed contrived. The fast runs, the excessive ornaments, and the dotted rhythms made you suspect that you had to overcome something when playing. It was theatre, plain and simple. The overture, which, technically considered, was pretty difficult, ended in a fugue, another hurried, crammed full piece that never calmed down.

The woman shook her head and slowly, without the pedal, started to figure out fingerings and tempo. All the fast notes had to sound quicker than was noted down, that's what Kirkpatrick wrote in his version of the score; you played at breakneck speed toward the longer notes, as if you were in a hurry, as if you were looking forward to something and could not wait for it to happen. The child who wanted to leave home, who talked excitedly with girlfriends about the room they would rent together, who perhaps against her better judgment, perhaps to overcome her fear, wanted to storm ahead. Keen desire, that's what the overture was about. Desire with blinkers, or does every desire have those? The woman remembered the trips to the north with the four of them in the car crammed full with rubber boots and empty jam jars; how they took turns shouting what they were most looking forward to: picking mushrooms; swimming in the lake; seeing their neighbours again. The light. The dark house. The whole car had buzzed and shuddered with desire.

To find a good tempo she had to consult the only passages in which you could hear a steady progress, no matter how quickly it was cut short again. Staccato sixteenths, first performed by the bass and then by the upper voice that tried to restrain impetuous desire and to curb it. The sixteenths determined the pattern in which she had to fit the almost exalted chaos. If you couldn't long for something that lay in the future, if you no longer dared to look forward to something, you were lost.

The woman worked. The overture shaped up. Her thinking took place on two levels: under the concentrated attention to movement and sound, a summer scene emerged, clouded and overrun by intense garlands of notes.

Evening on the high mountain. The neighbour sits at his garden table. He stares across the bay at the house on the spit of land. His large hands lie motionless on the table. His wife gets out of the car, talks about the flock of sheep; she has someone with her who wants to see the new stable; she speaks to her husband; she comes closer. He doesn't move.

'Come with me for a moment,' she says, 'get up. What's the matter with you?'

Variation 16, overture

Slowly he turns his face under the knotted handkerchief toward her. 'They are not coming,' he says with difficulty. 'Something has happened. They are not coming.'

The ornaments demanded total attention, including the nasty little fugue that followed the overture. With clenched teeth she wrestled through the notes, clung to the upper layer of her consciousness, thought of the quick movements of her fingers, and thought of nothing, of nothing else.

∞

The father has rented a van. He honks impatiently in the parking spot, gets out and opens the garage doors. He looks critically at the collection of stuff that is piled up. A table. Moving boxes. A dressing table. Chairs. Suitcases. A stack of saucepans. Buckets. A framed mirror. The daughter enters the garage with a pile of coats in her arms. She collapses on a kitchen chair and buries her head in the pile of coats. Muffled groaning.

'Dad! Help me!'

'I'm just thinking how to load it,' says the father. 'The boxes aren't closed properly. We'll make two trips. Do you have everything here?'

'I don't know. Mum's still busy with kitchen things. It's so much! It doesn't matter, does it?'

'Just make sure everything's here, then I can size it up.'

He pulls open the back door of the van and busies himself with blankets and supports. The daughter goes into the garden and talks to the rabbit sitting near the front of the hutch with its nose pressed against the chicken wire. She bends down to pull a dandelion leaf from the ground.

'Here, for you, just eat it. I'll come back every week to feed you.' Sobbing, she runs into the house through the open garden doors, up the stairs to her room.

The mother sits on the bed and looks around. She is wearing an old shirt. 'It's so bare now,' she says. The daughter, still sobbing, sits down next to her.

'I'm taking all the beautiful things. The important things.'

Empty shelves in the bookcase. Light areas on the walls where the posters used to hang.

'We'll paint it,' says the mother, 'Then it will be nice again, pleasant to come back to. Downstairs I've packed a box with plates and glasses and things for you. And this week we'll go and buy sheets together. Towels.'

'Are you angry?' asks the daughter.

The mother is silent. Yes, she is furious; she is horrified that this is really happening and that she has to help as well. She is stuck in her resistance—there is no way out. She wants to restrain the daughter—it's too soon, you are too young—but resists these feelings. She wants to be happy that the child aspires to an independent existence, to be proud of her enterprising spirit, the courage that is revealed by her move, but feels anger and opposition when she thinks of it.

'It's a nice house. It's great for you. And nice with these girls. It's also unpleasant that you're leaving. Sad.'

The daughter jumps up and stomps on the floor. 'They're all going away. That's how it should be, Mum! It's NOT awful.' She has tears in her eyes. The mother sighs and shifts her position. She feels something against her thigh, lifts off the blankets and sees the doll.

The girl snatches the doll from the bed and presses it against her. She leaves the room. The mother hears the dragging footsteps on the stairs, the garage doors banging shut, the increasing drone of the van's engine.

Variation 17

The neighbour is standing on the platform. With his tall frame he towers over the others who are waiting. The girl sees him as soon as the train draws into the station. She squeezes her friend's arm.

'Look, there, the one with the handkerchief on his head, he's come to pick us up. So sweet!' She jumps off the train and waving a large bag, she rushes up to the waiting man. The boyfriend, shy, follows at a distance.

'Well,' says the neighbour, 'here you are for once without your parents. How do you like the student life in Stockholm? Hard?'

The girl giggles. 'Hard partying. I haven't really studied much. What's happened here? It looks so different.' In the square of the provincial city, the three of them stand looking around.

'Another season,' says the neighbour. 'You've always been here in the middle of the summer. Now the trees are a lighter green. No tourists. The shops close earlier.'

During the trip to the house on the mountain, the girl chatters in different languages. She tells the neighbour in Swedish that she turned twenty-five the previous week; to her friend she points out in Dutch a dark path in the woods that always frightened her as a child because she knew for sure that scary trolls lived there; and then, flushing, she switches to English so everyone can understand the conversation.

When she arrives, she embraces the neighbour's wife and valiantly endures the dogs' greeting.

'Where are the sheep? May we sleep outside tonight? At the lake? Can we swim already, or is it still freezing cold?'

'Preferably in the hayloft,' the neighbour suggests, 'that's more protected. There are no mosquitoes yet.'

'Yeah, down below, near our old house!' She points out to her friend a long and narrow wooden barn that lies below, at the bay. Sheep are grazing on the pasture in front of it.

She can't sit still. Every other minute she has to get up from the table and run out of the kitchen to check the strawberry beds or to lean against the flagpole from where there is a great view of the spit of land below. After the meal she sits next to the neighbour on the steps, smoking a cigarette.

'You're like your mother,' he says. 'I always used to sit here with her. Identifying mushrooms. Talking about music.'

She has already jumped to her feet, and the neighbour hears her in the kitchen talking with his wife. Where should she put away the dried knives, may they take a torch with them down below, will the sheep corner her when she takes a pee in the meadow during the night? The boyfriend walks slowly across the land. He is silent.

Inside they drink more wine. The neighbour takes a photo of the couple, leaning against the kitchen counter and against each other. Everyone laughs. Then they pull on their rubber boots and pick up the sleeping bags.

'Brush your teeth here,' says the neighbour, 'then at least that's taken care of.'

Her husband walks down with them. On the path between the juniper berries, every rock, every blade of grass can be seen clearly.

'Do the sheep get confused if it's always light?' asks the boyfriend. He has placed his hand on the girl's neck. The hay barn looms up black and high at the end of the road. The neighbour prises open the tall door; it is unexpectedly dark inside. They climb up carefully on creaking ladders, across stacked hay bales, with the torch. The hayloft is completely open to the side of the meadow. The neighbour cuts loose the twine of a few bales and spreads the hay over the layer underneath.

'This way you'll be comfortable.' The girl lies down to check it. 'I can see your house from here!'

'Give us an SOS signal with the torch if there's trouble.'

'What are you talking about?' says the boyfriend. 'Isn't it safe here?'

No one answers. In the silence the grinding jaws of the sheep can be heard, the fierce little tugs with which they bite off the grass, the sigh of the girl.

The neighbour leaves. They watch him go, see how he walks down the path with buoyant steps until he disappears in the darkness of the wood's edge.

'Tomorrow I'll show you our house. No one lives there anymore. Everything here is empty. We're alone. There, in the woods next to the meadow, is the fish-hawk's nest. You'll see it tomorrow when we go swimming.'

She wakes up in the very early morning. The light has become changed, greyer. The sheep stand and sleep in a shallow sea of mist trails. Carefully she extracts herself from the bedding, clambers down past the snoring boy and leaves the barn. On the path to the black house stands a small animal, a dog she thinks, no, it's a young fox that looks at her with bright, friendly eyes before disappearing into the grass. She walks around the house, and at every window she stands on tiptoe to look inside. The kitchen where she made raspberry jam with her mother, the large hall where she played shepherd with her brother, the open fireplace where she built fires with her father. The steps at the back where the angry giant bee used to live. My whole childhood, she thinks, it's nothing actually, nothing that you can explain, nothing special. And yet it's everything. I'll show it to him. But will he be able to see it?

When she returns to the hayloft, he is sitting bolt upright.

'This place is crawling with vermin! I saw a mouse!'

'You should see my place. In Amsterdam I've raised dozens of mouse families. I'm an expert! Come, we're going swimming.'

∞

The restlessness of Variation 17 worried her; tensed like a spring, she was trying to restrain the tempo. It threatened to run away with her, especially in the long, descending sequences without a clear melodic line. It was pure movement; it invited you to run along.

She decided to do without Kirkpatrick's indications this time. To play what is written down, to let the hands find their way across and over each other, touch the keys gently but quickly, and immediately lift the fingers to make way for a new touch. The whole piece whispering, perhaps with the left pedal, at any rate with the sound as restrained as possible. Toward the end flare up quickly, give a little more at that high C, the highest note of the whole variation? If only it didn't sound too loud, thought the woman. It should not become expressive but should remain sheer rustling. Strange to have at your disposal such an enormous grand piano on which you could render running hippos and onrushing elephants but instead choose the small feet of mice.

Every sixteenth in the one voice had its opposite in the other. In counterpoint, practically everywhere. Every sound is connected to another sound. Every step that you take you will repeat one more time. What did that mean? There was no verdict about this. It only let us hear that it was this way, that the present and the past were glued to each other and would never come apart. No resonance, no tone, only entwining and breathless movement. She did not need to feel or to experience anything if she just played the notes accurately and restrainedly, tapped, softly, so that the sound disappeared again immediately. Yes.

Variation 18, canon at the sixth

Glenn Gould did not like to appear on stage. The piano concerto, which he experienced as a struggle between orchestra and keyboard, was an abomination to him. He didn't feel any more positively about the recital, during which, alone on the stage with his grand piano, he felt scrutinised and judged. Perhaps he felt most free on the organ bench, hidden behind the organ front and with his back to the nave of the church.

The woman had been absorbed with amazement in the programmes of his rare piano recitals. Hindemith, Haydn, Krenek, Schönberg. Surprised, she read that Gould would sometimes play all the canons of the Goldberg Variations one after the other, capped by the quodlibet. Strange that this solitary, socially fearful man chose from the range of Variations precisely those pieces that provided a sample of how two people could relate to each other. Imitate, support, contradict each other; take a harmonious or a dissonant point of view; walk away from each other or blend together, but

Variation 18, Canon at the Sixth

always in inevitable involvement with each other. Maybe he never felt it like that, thought the woman, maybe the music actually protected him against this kind of wishy-washy insight. The liberating thing about music is precisely that you can let go of limiting, depressing words and instead start thinking in sounds, in lines, in chords. Nothing needs to be put into words or translated.

She became absorbed in the canon at hand that obviously lay within the spectrum of consonance. The sixth is a sweet interval. The second voice, which imitates the first one in sixths, does not contradict but gives a loving, uncritical echo with a hint of sadness. She became so totally involved in playing the two voices in a clearly defined way that she was not aware of the meaning of the bass; it ambled along in an unstoppable cadence and unobtrusively kept everything together by its unassuming presence.

∞

'What now?' says the daughter when they leave the bank. 'Don't think we're going to talk; I've already done that with Dad. Everything will be different. I *know* it. Thanks. For the money.'

It is a grey, drizzly day. It isn't raining, yet faces and hair become damp and the paving stones turn dark grey.

'Good,' says the mother. 'We've discussed it long enough. Now you can start again with a clean slate. What do you feel like doing? Look in stores, have coffee, walk through the open-air market?'

The girl looks in the direction of the stalls. 'Yuck. You can tell from here that it stinks of fish. And too many people.'

Resolutely they go the other way. They cross the river, laugh at the name of a ship, "Everything is temporary," and eventually end up in the botanical garden.

'Yes,' says the daughter, 'this is great! Look, they have a plant doctor here, I can come with my cactus during office hours.'

Behind the narrow entrance gate there is a wood of dark green, shiny trees. There isn't a soul. They wander around; here and there place their hand on a tree trunk and glance at the signs that are set in the ground. In the palm house they climb up a narrow spiral staircase to look into the jungle from above. You can walk alongside it on a narrow plank bridge from which you look straight down. They don't do that. Downstairs there is a small bench next to an artificial waterfall. The girl discovers goldfish in the pond. They sit. They breathe warm, humid air.

'Do you still remember how we used to go and look at the *Victoria amazonica*?' asks the mother. 'It flowered at night. It smelled of pineapple.'

'You're always talking about the past. It's the present, you know.'

In the distance people are coming in. A door bangs shut. Mother and daughter look at each other and stand up at the same time. Determined, the girl walks to the exit; the mother follows in her footsteps. Outside, the daughter points at a small hothouse that stands at the side of the path.

'Look, flesh-eating plants. I remember that we found them in Sweden. They stood in a small bowl on the table and we gave them dead mosquitoes while we ate. Otherwise it was pitiful.'

'Shall we take a quick look?'

The girl shakes her head. She continues walking to the back of the garden where there is a long, narrow hothouse. A sign hangs on the door: "No entry. Butterfly house."

They go inside. It is warm, but drier than in the palm house. A summer-like heat. Numerous flowering plants stand in the boxes along the sides. It smells sweet, with a hint of rot.

Variation 18, canon at the sixth

It is so quiet that they hear water dripping from a tap. The mother walks past the fragrant flowers. Suddenly she turns around, as if wondering where the girl's footsteps have gone.

The girl stands stock still on the narrow tile path. Her arms hang next to her body and she has closed her eyes. Around her face fly large, dark butterflies. Purple, dark red, rust. One lands on her forehead, right near the hairline. Another flutters against her cheek. The girl smiles. The butterflies cover her hands, her ears, her neck.

The mother suddenly feels tears well in her eyes. She clasps the edge of the plant box tightly and looks for a long time at the daughter who is being kissed by butterflies.

Variation 19

What to do on a Sunday afternoon in the autumn? It's a nasty autumn; chilly rain strikes façades and paving stones; the sky is cloudy and dark. Their heads down, people walk across bridges and canals on their way to museums or concert halls. In the entrance hall of the cultural centre that used to be a courthouse, visitors stomp the dirt from their shoes and shake out their umbrellas. Still shivering, they enter the café through the glass doors. There the temperature is comfortable, and the murmuring voices and the tinkling glasses stir pleasant expectations. A literature programme in the small hall, but first a glass of wine; that's all right by this time—it's four o'clock; a red wine—after all, it's cold.

A pimply young man dressed in black and with a ponytail, opens the door to the hall and stands next to it to check the tickets. The audience comes flocking in: greying couples, women in their late forties with shawls and boots, older students carrying briefcases with perhaps an unpublished manuscript, lively young women with cold, red cheeks. More chairs have to be brought in; it's full today.

The host of the programme is an erudite, caustic critic. Together with two colleagues, he will go over and discuss the books published in the previous month. The three of them will determine what is literature and what is not, so the public won't get strange ideas. They will be stern, but they will do justice to the literary rules. He rubs his hands, knocks the microphone off the table and welcomes the audience.

For a whole hour learned opinions and sarcastic comments fly through the hall. Books of poetry are thrown back on the table with contempt, novels decisively relegated to the rubbish bin. A single prose poem by an unknown author receives a response that could, with some effort, be considered satisfactory. The speakers bombard each other fast and furiously with literary categories, linguistic philosophy and the art of perspective. In closing, they are satisfied that once again there was nothing of worth his month. The host announces a break.

'To let you catch your breath, we have something special this afternoon. A band. Young people, students. They are going to entertain you. You may leave the hall to get a drink and you may bring the glass back with you. I would do that because we have a wonderful singer. Here she is. Please welcome her!'

He sinks back into his chair, exhausted, and begins leafing through the books and papers near the edge of the table. The band members grab their instruments and their music stands. A sudden, loud beep comes from the sound system. More than half of the audience has left.

The musicians are now standing next to the table. Drums, bass, keyboard, and a shy girl with a guitar. In front of them, at the microphone, stands the singer. She is wearing dark grey slacks, sneakers, and a short-sleeved T-shirt. Her bare arms look plump and solid at the same time, like those of a young child. She has fastened her hair in a small bun at the back of her head. Looking serious, she lifts the microphone out of its stand. She looks back, makes eye contact with all her colleagues and gives a brief nod. Then the music bursts forth.

The people on their way to the exit slow down and turn around. The hall is filled with powerful simple chords, above which the song line coils smoothly and gracefully. The musicians devote themselves to the song; the concentration on their faces captures the attention of the listeners. In its simplicity, the sound seems to sweep the profusion of complex words and ideas out of the hall. The contrast between the literary discussion and the freshness of the music makes the musicians seem even younger than they are.

The singer is enjoying herself. She moves with a fast rhythm and expresses the lively words perfectly. With a smile and a childlike gesture she invites the various band members for their solos. She takes a step back and follows what they do with interest. Then she steps forward again and belts out the last refrain forcefully and fast. Applause. One or two people cheer. The host, who now has a glass of beer, moves papers from one stack to the other.

The band members sit down behind the stage. The guitarist pushes her chair forward so that she sits next to the singer. The girl stands up straight, her head bowed, waiting for silence. Conversations fall silent; a chair leg moves crunching across the floor; someone kicks against a glass and it falls over.

After the power of the previous number, the guitar chords sound thin and careful; the sound disappears immediately after the touch; the listeners prick up their ears so they can follow the line. The singer closes her eyes and brings the microphone so close to her mouth that her lips touch the metal. She holds it with both hands; she keeps her arms, which a moment ago moved wildly and waved rhythmically all around her, close to her body. She starts singing softly, and suddenly the hall is so quiet that the walls seem to come closer with nothing else but the intimate space in which the girl weaves her song. The words are about meeting a boy—how he was, what he said. Her voice is restrained and sad, but these signs are already too much. With subtle rhythmic shifts she dances across the steady cadence of the guitar. She places the high points as a matter of course and naturally, but still quietly and softly. For the whole song she remains within the spectrum of the unassuming sound. She introduces nuances and accents not with a big sound but with marvellous phrasing.

The audience is captivated by her quiet oval face with its delicate eyelids. The listeners don't wonder about what is happening here but are engrossed in the sound. The tenderness toward the young, eager musicians has ebbed away. This sounds serious. The host has placed his hands on the stacks of paper and listens. Where is the lively, enthusiastic girl he invited to come and sing? On the stage stands someone with wisdom, detachment, and dedication. On the stage stands a woman.

∞

Three-eight time. Three voices. The theme first in the middle voice, in sixteenths. A minuet? The second beat of every measure seems slightly heavier: a sarabande? Not too fast at any rate. And not too loud. Try to play the theme, in which every fourth measure is taken over by another voice, as if it were plucked on a guitar, all the notes detached, not snapped off, but simply separate. An exercise in varying one's touch.

That is what the woman thought. She liked this unpretentious piece, this timid dance. She heard the three voices and their relationship to one another in her head and tried to train her fingers so that they could do justice to this image. In some editions, it said "for the lute" above Variation 19. Bach was not referring to the instrument but to the harpsichord register with that name. If you pulled out that stop, the tone became muted, intense, intimate.

She had to place this piece in the sequence of variations; she must not get lost in what she was working on, but be aware of the straightforward and melodious singing that had sounded before and the wild outbursts that would follow. It wasn't easy to remain restrained in the dynamic, to indicate the melody line with tempo and rhythm, rather than with variations in volume. The piece tempted her time and again to make more sound than she actually wanted to. Halfway through the second part, she could no longer sustain the steady guitar touch and played for four measures with a strong legato, perhaps not more loudly than the rest, but completely legato, so that the notes rang out more. In the last four measures she resumed the guitar imitation.

Restrain. Never loosen the reins. Bend close to the keyboard. Let the fingers do their work lightly and surely. Hold back whatever sorrow welled up, ornament it with the muted guitar sounds, finish playing this intimate song calmly and without fear.

Variation 20

The light of the piano lamp formed a protective circle in which score, keyboard and hands were captured. The adjustment required precision. If the head of the lamp was turned too much toward the score, it created a shadow line on the keys that made you distracted. Too far the other way and the lamp shone in your eyes. If it was adjusted too high, then you saw nothing; if it was too low, you banged your head against it when you bent over the keys.

Before she started to play, the woman took the time to bring the lamp into a perfect position, like a warder who checks the cell walls for things that are out of place and then closes the cell door. Except that she remained inside. Except that the walls were made of light. Except that no limit had been set for the sentence.

Behind the jail walls rose the shadow where matters of increasing horror were hiding. There was the expanse of the room where the table stood prominently with its load of papers, books, and photos. There were windows behind her back, invisible. Beyond these windows was the world that everyone put up with, a world where it was NOW, where traces of the past were easily erased, façades looked forward to new paint, and trees longed for spring.

Spring in the past was one thing. Who knows, it might have been spring in Bach's head when he composed the twentieth variation with all those cheerful ascending triads, continually sprinkled by staccato raindrops performed by the other hand. Babbling brooks from which the water splashed, pushed forward, burst forth jubilantly and cascaded in a frothing stream. Brooks that dragged along the winter's rubbish, rotten leaves, abandoned birds' nests, thrown out papers. The water swirled, dragged along everything that was loose in a springtime flush, in a healthy intoxication that knew its limits. Thirty-two measures, no more.

During her practice she thought of the world outside. As long as her fingers were connected to the keys she felt safe enough. From deep within her there emerged a scent, a scent of water in the evening. The boys in the neighbourhood were shouting; she had gone outside, aware of the existence of a world outside the walls of the house. They were playing in a meadow, stood talking on a small road with round cobblestones with grass growing in between. This will become life, she had thought then with her small girl's brain, this and much, much more. I can wander around in this magnificence for the rest of my life. It had been an almost solemn feeling, for which she hadn't had any words then, but which now surfaced perfectly intact.

She turned her back to the world and started to practise the triads and the bubbling triplets.

∞

Variation 20

'Tell me, tell me!' says the mother.

The boy hoists his suitcase onto a cart and gives her a sidelong glance.

'Wild,' he says, 'I haven't slept for two weeks! It's going great there. Really great.' He puts his arm around the mother's shoulder. Slowly they push the trolley across the parking area of the airport.

In the car he stretches and yawns. 'She was really happy that I came. We slept together in her room. *If* we slept at all. It smelled just like her house here. Twenty students live in one hall, and they all share the kitchen. The Swedish way—everyone has his own refrigerator. They stand along the walls; can you imagine, a bank of twenty refrigerators! There's an enormous table in the middle of the kitchen, and we climbed on it to sing.'

The boy smiles and slumps back. The car bores through the fog; outside the warm, swaying car everything is grey.

'We also had a sausage party. It lasted three days! And we went to expensive discos in Stockholm with small bottles of vodka in our pockets. It didn't stop. A party every day. Mostly we stayed on campus. Nothing but foreigners, so speaking Swedish didn't really happen. She sings in a choir—of course that's in Swedish. It's good—I went with her to a rehearsal. Everything by heart!' He hums a tune, beats out a rhythm on his thighs.

'I don't think she has any worries there. She's relaxed. Studying is too much right now—she doesn't do it. Look, just doing the laundry is quite an undertaking. You have to book a time for a machine in one of those strange basements. We set the alarm for it—really early in the morning we traipse through the snow with bags full of stinky clothes. Forgot the detergent, went back, ran out of change, to the office that was closed—it just didn't work. By the time we finished the preparations, the next person in line for laundry was tapping on his watch. We did laugh a lot.

'She organised the badminton world championship. That was an amazing feat. So typical of her, getting all these foreigners together. French, Austrians, Finns, everyone who lives on that campus in a large sports centre, with small flags and each country with its own colour shirt. We hid the liquor in the dressing room lockers because you aren't allowed to drink there. We stood on the stands, yelling and screaming, no matter who played. She wrote the results on a blackboard. The Spanish were super-fanatic, and they did win, as far as we could tell. And everyone constantly had to sing their national anthem, win or lose. One of these very proper Swedish caretakers came in to check what all the racket was about. She winds the man around her little finger; before you knew it he was also cheering on the sidelines. I'm pretty much done for.'

The mother turns off the freeway. They drive between meadows where cows stand in the fog.

'The best thing was: together in her room. Just like it used to be. Once a week, on Tuesday, everyone opens their window, at exactly six o'clock. Then they start screaming. As loud as they can. All these red faces sticking out of the windows. The sound echoes. Concrete walls, you know. We hung out of her window, together. We looked at each other and couldn't stop laughing. We'd ended up someplace where everything and everyone was stark raving mad, and yet we felt totally at ease. I'm really going to sleep for three days, right now.'

The mother steers the car through the low-hanging clouds. Next to her the son falls asleep.

∞

The world behind the windows seemed to pull on the woman and prevented absolute concentration on her work. Perhaps "pull" was too strong a word and it was more a question of an annoying fluctuation of attention because of a certain tugging at her consciousness, because of the disturbing idea that outside the circle of light, outside Bach, all sorts of presences were waiting. For her.

She shrugged her shoulders. Out of the question that she would turn her back to the keyboard, that she would direct her gaze outside. Here, in the warm yellow light of the piano lamp, here was where it happened. Here she could let a girl dance in a sports centre in Stockholm, here she brought inside what was outside. Expand, she thought. Remain within the circle of light but still search for a wider horizon. Beyond Bach? Why shouldn't she learn something else, in addition to the Goldberg Variations—a Chopin etude, a Brahms sonata, something by Ravel? The entire piano repertoire lay patiently in the music cabinet, all she needed to do was to get up and rummage in the stacks for something to her liking. She did not get up. She remained sitting within the walls of light and played Variation 20.

Variation 21, canon at the seventh

She thought about contrasts. The Goldberg Variations were technically difficult to play and therefore other difficulties were concealed. One of those was the enormous contrast between one variation and the other. She had just now played number 20, fast, alert, steering her attention from one hand to the other at every measure, almost toppling over in the bubbling triplet passages when she really had to make sure at every note that the finger used to strike it was pulled back in time, even faster than you could think; with every plunge in the depth she had to anticipate the next leap, every standstill carried breathless running inside it.

Immediately afterwards came the slow-moving canon at the seventh. In a minor key, slow, tranquil. Was this the variation that Glenn Gould during his first recording played, by his own account, like a nocturne by Field? The woman could easily imagine it. A cautiously ascending line that descended again immediately and practically demanded a rubato. Hesitant steps in minor seconds that you could not

Variation 21, canon at the seventh

play without dramatic tempo changes. Stumbling, climbing, hurtling down, that sort of thing.

Why does a melody that ascends and then descends make us feel so sad? Had Bach made any headway when he knew this? A hopeful inhale, a disappointed exhale. Uphill, and then, inevitably, downhill. Obtaining something and then having to give it up again. Life itself, therefore. Hence the lump in your throat. You could analyse measure by measure precisely how Bach managed to do it. Dozens of philosophical musical treatises must have been written about this. You could not call it science; the emotion felt at this Variation did not disappear when you encountered somewhere in the world a melody that ascended, descended, and left you cold. This Variation did not let itself be negated by any counterexample.

Put a stop to this, she thought. Stop analysing and thinking. But what then? She *had* to think, even if only about the exceptional interval between the postulating and the answering voice: a seventh! It should sound harrowing, contrary and uneasy, but the voices joined together smoothly and gave each other space instead of thwarting each other. Stop thinking. It explained nothing.

Her hands lay in her lap. She wanted to be filled with the sound that chased away all words. Then it would be about what the song let her feel. She didn't need to explain it, only let it happen. There were no words for fear and panic, just as there were none for that other thing, for that which the song expressed. Now play and let the melody live. She waited. Come on, she thought, do it. She moved her hands to the keyboard. After two measures there was an end to the experiment. Her vision became cloudy and blurred so that she could no longer distinguish the notes. She snapped shut the score and turned off the lamp.

∞

The mother walks through the city, along canals, across bridges, with sunglasses on her nose, holding a carry bag from a dress shop. This is the daughter's domain. There, across the street, is the institute where she studies. In the alley next to it is the café where the mother has sat countless times with her to eat giant slices of cake and to listen to excited stories about fellow students and instructors. Maybe she was just here, thinks the mother, maybe her bicycle is standing next to this bridge. She scrutinises the saddles and the locks; she turns her eyes to the ground when she realises what she is doing.

Distance, she thinks. A twenty-six-year-old child is an adult, has her own life, should not share every setback and every decision with her mother. But she needs me, thinks the mother, last night she sounded awful on the telephone, insecure and sad. She didn't want to get together today. 'No, Mum, I'll figure it out myself. I've got no time anyway tomorrow.' Conversation concluded. Doubt created. Worry emerged.

How heavy my legs feel, thinks the mother, I'm dragging myself along, ridiculous. I need her. I act as if it's about her career choice, about the difficulty she will have after graduation in finding a direction. But I can't let go of her any more than she can of me. She wants to be on my lap and I want her to climb on my lap. That's how it is.

The windows of the dress shops display the summer collection. That dress, thinks the mother, exactly her colour, exactly the retro style that she will wear with flair. Her hand is ready to slip into her bag to get the phone. Jump on your bike, the mother wants to say, then you can try it on. Afterwards we'll have a cup of coffee. She restrains herself, leans against the bridge and puts her hands in her pockets.

There, in that café, isn't she sitting there? The daughter's profile, the ponytail, the gesturing hands, the smile that shows her teeth—there she is!

Variation 21, Canon at the Seventh

The mother wants to start running but restrains herself. She almost loses her balance. The hair is too dark, the shoulders too broad. Slowly she walks down from the bridge, away from the store filled with summer dresses, away from the deceptive image of the daughter. The stones are steel grey. They have carried the daughter's feet. The mother follows the invisible footsteps at a slow pace, with bowed head.

Variation 22, alla breve

The father parks the red car on the asphalt at the bottom of the dike. The children clamber up while the parents lift suitcases and backpacks from the trunk. The boy and the girl stand close together between the sheep and gaze across the sea to the island. His coat is red; hers is blue. A stiff wind blows their hair upwards; the force of the storm makes them laugh; they point out the waves with white crests and shout with excitement when the ferry docks.

Backpacks on. The father carries the suitcase. Hand in hand they march to the landing where a real captain in a fisherman's jumper checks the tickets. Across the gangplank, across the high metal speed bumps, getting dizzy from the smells: stale coffee, motor oil, salt.

'Where is the horn?' asks the boy with a hint of fear in his voice. The father lifts him up and holds him tightly until the signal for departure has sounded. The girl reaches up and strokes the brother's soft round calf.

'Isn't he sweet?' she says to her mother. 'He loves the horn and he's afraid of the horn.' She takes the boy by the hand as soon as his father sets him down on the deck. They run to the rail and look intently at the trail of foam that the boat pulls through the water.

The next day the four of them walk through the dark coniferous forest to the dunes. Cold wind and bright sun; the children have pulled the hoods of their coats over their heads and have tied them closed. Past the edge of the woods the landscape opens up in yellows and greys. Birds alight on a pool surrounded by dried reed tufts that are at least a metre and a half tall. The father cuts a few with his pocketknife. Then the two children parade one behind the other to the top of a dune. They lift the reed plumes high and clasp the thick stalks with both hands. The girl reaches the top first, turns toward her brother and stands on tiptoe. The mother looks at the pale oval of the little face encircled by the hood.

The children lift the reeds as high as they can; they dance on the dune top and let the reed plumes flutter in the wind like flags. The girl shouts: 'We see everything! We're standing on top of the world!'

∞

Alla breve, a 4/4 time that you have to feel and perform in two; it made you feel energetic. Not rushed, but instead purposeful, making good time, almost cheerful. A "nothing is the matter" feeling.

Calmly the woman examined the four voices that imitated each other loosely with descending intervals of fifths and turns after the first beat. All the four-part Goldberg Variations reminded her of holidays, of pleasant excursions within the safe shelter of the foursome. Here, in this Variation, the soprano part carried something invincible within it, the still uncomplicated instinct for discovery of a child who directed herself almost euphorically to the world. Still without reluctance, still looking at the world without soot-covered glasses. The other child followed her, in sixths, in thirds, even in the dizzying run uphill. He let her go at the reckless trill in measure eleven, to catch her again later in good spirits.

Below them the parents' low voices rumbled along contentedly. The imperturbable bass. The tenor that was silent for measures on end and then joined in again.

For a satisfactory performance it was better to let go of all references to meaning, thought the woman. Associations and memories created confusion and distracted from what was to become a pure play of lines. She knew that she could do it. If she concentrated with all her available energy on the parts, the images and the words would float to the background, and a pure structure would remain that referred to nothing, that only existed.

That trill was hopeless. Third and fourth finger of the right hand, holding your thumb on the third below; rhythmically independent of the lower voices; ending up at the right note exactly at the start of the next measure. A struggle.

She would like to open her ears wide, just as it was possible with eyes and nostrils. She would like to be all ears, and with those all-powerful ears suck in all the sound, into the treacherous brain. There the weave of voices would push everything aside: a child's blue jacket, a high-pitched girl's voice, blinding white clouds against a brilliant blue sky, an earsplitting ship's horn. In the skull, harmony would reign, nothing but harmony.

Variation 23

Around her tenth birthday, the child is finished, complete. Her gaze is directed at the world and the wonders in it; her existence is anchored solidly in the parental home. Her motor system is stable and reliable: bicycling, writing, skating, making music—no problem. The child makes distinctions between acquaintances, friends and a close friend. A world of play and fantasy exists next to the world of reality. Abstractions are still rooted in the concrete, powerlessness is not yet paralysing, death is understood but is not yet fathomed.

The child of ten is a joy in the house. She knows the rituals and looks forward to them. She tolerates deferral and makes the effort to reach a distant goal. She is content with herself and with her place in the class, in the family, at the table.

It is December—outside a chilly wind blows and inside the heater is roaring. She ties on an apron and drags a chair to the kitchen to take a mixing bowl from high up in the cupboard. The St. Nicholas celebration is over—new toys and new clothes; the Christmas holidays lie in the future, but now, as is proper in a half-Swedish environment, first is Lucia, the festival of light in the darkest time. She should actually be wearing a crown with candles and a white dress. But there are limits. 'I'm not doing that, I'll just get candle wax in my hair.'

They limit it to Lucia sweet rolls that they will bake now, in the evening, and will eat tomorrow morning before the first light.

'You look for the cookbook,' she says, and the mother pulls the stained book out of the cupboard. Newspaper clippings fall out and a dried sunflower as well. The page with the Lucia rolls is smeared with last year's dough. Delighted, the girl examines the complicated examples of shiny, entwined and braided dough.

'We need raisins,' she says. 'If you do the yellow stuff, I'll make the dough.' She cuts open a packet of bread mix and accurately measures a quantity of water into a jug. The mother crumbles the saffron tendrils into a soup bowl.

'Crocuses. The stamens of crocus flowers. They weigh nothing; it looks terrible, but it colours everything yellow.' The girl nods. She stirs water through the flour and starts to knead, giggling when the dough hangs from her fingers in lumps.

'I'd better not sneeze now, Mum!'

The mother flings a lump of butter into the bowl. The girl lets the fat squeeze though her fingers. Then the mashed saffron is added and mother and daughter watch how the dough becomes coloured. Orange flecks, yellow circles around them. The girl's small hands work it in efficiently and fold the dough slabs over each other again and again into a new lump that becomes more and more yellow.

'Well. Now it has to rest. With a cloth over it.' She covers the dough with a teatowel and carefully places the bowl on the heat register. She pushes her hands under the mother's nose. 'Smells nice, doesn't it?'

Variation 23

When it's time for the next round of kneading, she calls her brother. The mother sprinkles a film of flour over the kitchen table, looks for the rolling pin, lifts the orange ball of dough out of the warm bowl.

The boy examines the examples in the cookbook as he beats out a strong rhythm on his thighs. Soon they will divide the dough into small pieces and carefully shape the rolls—first according to the prescribed patterns with strange names (heavenly gate, priest's wig) and then according to their own designs: cars, aeroplanes, a tortoise, and an elk's head with fragile antlers. After that they will sit in front of the oven, with flour on their cheeks, to watch their sculptures rise and brown.

But first the last task, the final kneading. The lump of dough feels heavy and unmanageable. Even the mother's strong fingers can't get a grip on it.

'Give it to me, Mum,' says the boy. The mother sees him standing, crouched, arms lifted, like a goalie between the goalposts. She throws, he catches, bending with the weight of the ball. The girl jumps up, calls out and reaches for the golden yellow, warm orange ball of flour; they scream and laugh and run around. They keep the golden dough in the air like a sun; it doesn't dash against the bookcase, doesn't smash against the floor, but flies from one pair of hands to the other like a fiery, nutritious soccer ball, thrown with confidence, caught with care. Festival of light.

∞

She started on Variation 23 with limber fingers. She always used to start her practice with a solid half hour of technique: scales, every day in another key; triads, patiently through the circle of fifths; exercises for a limber wrist; octave passages for accuracy; scales in thirds and sixths; a few of the really difficult *Übungen für Klavier* by Brahms. That time was past; she was no longer in the mood for that technical misery. It had been a battle, day after day, a struggle with the piano which she now preferred to see as an ally. What had it availed her, that required daily exercise? A feeling of mastery. She was the master of these black and white bits of wood. Proud of the discipline that she managed to summon. Satisfaction. A certain technical benefit, because if she encountered scales somewhere in a sonata, the fingering was obvious, just as in brilliant passages filled with arpeggios. Except that everything in the reality of composed pieces always turned out a little different in the technical exercises. A chord position might be skipped, and in the runs a note was invariably added so that the whole thing no longer tallied. And yet.

You couldn't start the Goldberg Variations just like that. You had to practise, warm up the muscles. She picked up a Haydn sonata. Simple, slow sight-reading. Making as few mistakes as possible, choosing a tempo in which she could play it. Looking ahead. Feeling the fingers. Listening.

When she started on Variation 23, she had warmed up. The pleasure of movement that had started with Haydn stayed with her. She calmly made decisions about hand positions: the melody, in intervals, above, with a heavy hand; cascading ornaments with light fingers below. Nice scales in contrary motion, superfast. Halfway through the second part, the confusing cry of despair of the modulation to E minor, a sad small island in a sea of cheerfulness.

Then came the pounding thirds and sixths. Now it would be useful if the fingers stood in the correct position by themselves, trained according to the handbook by K.A. Textor (*Vingerzettingtabellen voor Dubbelgreeptoonladders*—fingering tables for double stop scales) that contained no notes but only numbers. But her fingers didn't do that. The measures with alternating thirds posed hardly any problems; she used the same fingering everywhere and saw in front of her bouncing, limber children who moved around each other and showed consideration for each other, *played*. The violence of the last two measures held her captive at the piano for hours. From the original playfulness, the innocence, there suddenly arose an ominous cascade of sound; a brilliant ascending passage of thirds, but under it began a descending run of sixths. In the last measure both voices ran to each other, raging, and then stopped suddenly in a short, restless final chord.

Variation 24, canon at the octave

This canon has an exceptionally dull theme, thought the woman. It dawdled on and on, voice after voice, in a wobbling three-part beat, like a couple of old people who move one behind the other with their walkers. You were absolutely sure that nothing at all was going to happen. A turn around the pond and then back into the nursing home. But it was Bach, it had the aura of sanctity, and that is why it was wrong to be cynical. She should consider the bridging function of this Variation to the virtuoso variation that she had just played and to the hushed lament that would follow it. She would have to practise this canon as intensely and with as much concentration as the other parts. It wasn't about the notes themselves but about your commitment to the notes. Because Bach was crazy about canons he must have loved this one a lot, this boring one that became beautiful because of his attention.

The woman had once stood in a toy store to buy a doll for the daughter who was about to turn six. She chose one made of a soft material, rubber or plastic, with blond hair like straw and a not unpleasant expression on a neutral face; simply a doll. When the girl received it (streamers, strawberry cake) she changed into a he, with hair trimmed distinctively by the daughter, a name, and an actual presence. The family began to see the doll as a housemate because the daughter's love had breathed life into it, just as Bach did with his canons.

She made fingerings. A pianist friend had recently asked her if she ever played anything else besides Bach, and what that was like. He himself was something of a Bach devotee, and they had at length exchanged ideas about the consequences of this. You would think that the subtle, finicky work in the centre of the keyboard would not help you very much when you subsequently plunged into the heavy Romantic repertoire. She had told him about a Brahms sonata that she was going to play with a cellist and that she had managed to get into her fingers surprisingly quickly—incomprehensible actually. Through a thorough study of Bach you became more aware of your fingers and you acquired a precision that you did not have before. It was also good for the ears; suddenly you heard in Chopin or in Brahms middle voices that you had always neglected. Content, they had smiled at each other. What did the friend think of the canon at the octave? In the Bach literature it was characterised as pastoral, gently rocking and idyllic, he said. The woman thought that was nonsense. The pianist agreed. No, it was not cheerful or calming. Instead a little sad. The woman went further and felt a threat in the last measures with the repeating, heavy notes. That's of course how it was meant; Bach prepared the ears and the feelings to experience the variation that follows.

Bach was much more intelligent than you could ever grasp; you would be happy just to play the notes that he had written down. The pounding bells of doom were prepared earlier in the piece by lighter touches in the same rhythm, on each beat of the measure. You had to play those with your little finger because the rest of the hand was busy with the canon voices. Bach had composed it in such a way that the right phrasing was produced naturally; you had to pull your little finger back in time, otherwise you couldn't play the melody. That had been thought of about three centuries ago.

The fact that the image of shuffling old folks occurred to her was no surprise because there was in the piece a relentlessly ticking clock that seemed inescapable at the end. The threat was not carried out, no hailstorm, no cerebral hemorrhage—just coffee in the nursing home cafeteria. Nothing the matter, false alarm. The elderly basked in false safety and let their wildly beating hearts quiet down at the formica table with its fake flower arrangement.

She smiled. Then her face became serious, and she began to play the canon at the octave intently.

∞

This winter holidays are a horror, a mistake. They travelled to the farthest North, to a deserted, mountainous area where it is a freezing minus twenty degrees Celsius and where even in the middle of the day there is no light. The children play in the snow, they slide down the gentle slopes on sleds and small skis and then scramble back up, laughing and stumbling. The friends with whom they are staying are preparing an elk stew; in the workshop the father wraps an ice-hockey stick for the son. Shivering, the mother smokes a cigarette on the white porch. The daughter climbs on a pile of snow. Her boot becomes stuck between concealed boulders. She falls. She falls.

In the ambulance the mother sits right against the stretcher where the daughter lies. Her leg is secured in an orange cuff, filled with air. The mother holds the girl's thin hand tightly.

In her head the images of the past hour whirl in confusion: the screaming child on the ground; the oddly twisted leg; the serious face of the host who determinedly kicks open the part of the front door that is always closed. The unusual width of this entrance through which the ambulance drivers enter stomping, and through which they later, carefully, carry the child out to the waiting ambulance. The hypodermic needle with its saving morphine, the sickening smell of stewed elk meat.

Through the slits above the ambulance blinds, the mother looks at the night, at the black spruce trunks flashing by, at the reflection of moonlight on the frozen river. It is a long trip. The hospital is a little more than an hour's drive away. The daughter has dozed off.

White-clad men and women in white clogs are waiting at the emergency room. They take the daughter with them. They roll the child just like that into a hallway, through a door, gone. The mother runs after them; she demands a lead apron; she stays with the child when everyone withdraws behind a protective partition. Only when the x-rays are ready does the mother join the doctors. Silently they examine the lightbox on which a composition in black and grey is displayed, an image of the awful spiral-shaped fracture of the femur.

'Set it,' says the doctor. 'Traction. Fortunately the epiphyses are intact. If something goes wrong, she will correct it herself. How old is she? Nine? Good. We're going to operate immediately. When did she eat?'

They stand in a cluster in the hallway around the stretcher with the morphine-numbed daughter. The father, who has driven behind the ambulance, joins them. The mouths of the parents each whisper into one of the girl's ears: broken leg; the doctor will fix it; it will be fine. The mother consults with a tall nurse; a bed will be pulled into the children's ward so that she can lie next to the daughter after the operation and can tell her what has happened when she wakes up.

'Mummy, will I sleep here?'

'Yes, you have to stay here for a while. I'm getting a bed next to you.'

The doctor nods. The white-clad nurses get ready to roll the stretcher away. The surgeon has already gone to the operating theatre.

'The doctor will make you sleep very soon. When you wake up, I will be with you.'

The girl seems overwhelmed; she looks back and forth from the mother to the father, and it is clear from her face that she wants to ask all sorts of things, but she only sighs.

After the operation the father will drive back to pick up various things—the toothbrush, for example, and a favorite book, jumpers, and puzzles—'the doll,' mother and daughter say simultaneously. Yes that too, that especially. Tomorrow morning the father will bring the doll.

With her elbow the nurse presses a button on the wall, and the doors to the operating room open.

'You have to say goodbye here,' she says. Petrified, the parents remain standing in front of the closing panels, staring at the slowly rolling stretcher that disappears behind the frosted glass.

It is not completely dark in the children's ward. The door is ajar and lets a band of light fall on the linoleum. A weak light burns above the daughter's bed. The windows shine like dark ice. On the far side of the ward lies a strange child who moans and sometimes even cries fretfully. The child's mother is there, a plump woman who sat up startled when the child was rolled into the ward and who is now snoring. From time to time the band of light widens, and a nurse enters and sweeps over the girl with the light of a torch. She checks the drip. She skirts around the lead weights that hang on the traction apparatus behind the foot of the bed. She

Variation 24, canon at the octave

casts a glance at the mother who pretends to be sleeping. She disappears into the hallway.

It is warm. The mother is exhausted but can't sleep. She doesn't want to sleep. Soon the child will wake up and discover that the doctor has driven a steel pin straight through her knee. The ends of the pin are fastened in a bracket. Cables run from the bracket to a pulley fastened on to a traction system that towers above the bed. Weights pull the cables taut. The mother stares at the scaffolding in the scanty light. The daughter lies on her back; she can't do otherwise. She will be scared, will scream, faint in panic, throw up out of fear, choke with anger. The mother will have to be strong, will have to create a story with a beginning and an end from this nightmare, will have to give an overview, will have to overcome her own fear and not just push it aside.

She sits straight up in the ridiculous hospital bed and forces herself to breathe deeply and calmly while looking at the scaffolding. She registers her thoughts: the child is broken; someone has on purpose shot a steel pin through her perfect knee so that the complicated joint with its muscles, tendons, blood vessels and bones is suddenly present in a frightening and unseemly way; the girl is chained, and will be that way for months, among well-meaning people who don't understand her language.

The child is broken. The mother sighs in agitation. The mother rouses her mind. Pulling apart pieces of bone, setting the leg at the right length, waiting until the fracture planes find each other again in a cloud of callus—the only option, nothing special; it happens everywhere, every day. The pin through the knee.

She worries for no good reason; the girl will wake up and accept the explanation without difficulty. She will stay in the ward for three months, with her doll, and let her leg heal slowly. The father will stay with her when the mother and the brother have to go home to go to work and to school. The daughter will receive packages and letters from them. Sometimes she will be furious, will wet her bed, refuse food, and then again cheerfully play a game with the child across the room, write a letter to her class at school, joke with her visitors. In the occupational therapy department where they roll her with bed and traction apparatus, she cheerfully weaves the potholders that the mother still has in the kitchen.

The mother waits, but at this latitude there is no dawn. Soon she will have to say something.

Variation 25, adagio

The woman was absorbed in Bach's tragic death. Seen from the perspective of current medical knowledge, the composer's end was a succession of missed diagnoses, therapies bordering on quackery and interventions that could simply be called maltreatment. He did not complain—perhaps because he experienced no discomfort, perhaps because any discomfort was covered by his zest for work and musical fulfillment. Bach did not become worried until his sight was affected and he first had blurred vision and then saw hardly at all. More light, more candles on the work table, a forest of waxen stalks under flames swaying back and forth in the draft. Candle wax on the scores, scorch marks on the cuffs of his coat. His wife rummaged in chests and cupboards, searching for more candleholders, in despair because of her husband's angry shouts. You've ruined your eyes because of all your close work; you have to rest your eyes because they are tired.

He was in his mid-sixties, a strong, energetic man who gave lessons all day long, played the organ and led rehearsals.

In the evening he wanted to note down the ideas that he'd had to remember during the day for lack of time, and to continue working on his compositions. Irritated, he enlisted his sons, one or two reliable pupils, and maybe even his wife to help. When they couldn't keep up with his dictating speed or didn't understand, he pulled the paper towards him and scribbled the themes between the lines himself. Straggly, uneven, wrong. Perhaps, she complained to her grown stepsons in the hallway or in the kitchen: 'Help your father, I can't, it's too much for me. Go in, take over from him, he's ill.'

These days every family doctor would immediately check the blood sugar level and ask specifically about other symptoms: Weight loss? Frequent urination? Always thirsty? Anna Magdalena did not make the connection between the heavy chamber-pot that she carried down the stairs every morning to empty in the courtyard and her husband's complaints about his eyes. If she noticed that he was losing weight, that was a reason for her to feed him larger quantities of roasted meat and starchy foods. Then the poorly healing wounds on his feet that prevented him from regularly wearing his new shoes would surely heal faster. When he mentioned thirst, she ordered more beer. She took good care of her husband and led him unknowingly to the abyss.

He suffered from adult diabetes, linked to or caused by lack of physical movement—from his house to his work he did not need to take more than forty steps, and he exerted himself physically only when he climbed the steps to the organ—by eating a lot and a great deal of fat, drinking large quantities of alcohol, and smoking pipe tobacco. The kidneys gave out; the blood vessels were no longer equal to the task; and the nerves, in particular the valuable optical nerve, were affected. His blood was sweet and sticky like honey. Bach and his wife had no idea of the disintegration of the organism that kept the family, the city of Leipzig and the musical life of Europe going. He saw poorly; more candles were needed.

An English eye specialist came, a travelling healer with a suitcase filled with shiny instruments; he gave a talk about his surgical feats and with that offered Bach a solution. The operation cost a fortune; success seemed assured. The doctor drove up in his carriage that had wide-open eyes painted over its entire surface. Anna Magdalena welcomed him at the front door and led him, followed by two assistants, upstairs to the library.

The woman shuddered but could not stop the sinister thoughts, fascinated as she was by the contrast between the abstract, sublimated Variation 25 and the concrete pain and horror of the operation. She saw before her how the assistants moved the wide chair with the armrests to the window and pushed a pillow against the headrest where Bach had to place his head. Did they tie his arms to the armrests with leather straps? Anyway, the doctor made several incisions with a small knife, first in one eye and then in the other. With a small brush he wreaked havoc under the cornea, and to top off his work he insisted on copious bleeding. He left behind a shocked and weakened patient. Anna Magdalena was in the kitchen throwing up with misery and was incapable of bidding farewell to the healer. After a day the bandage could be removed, and for a short while it looked as though the composer had regained his eyesight. He staggered when he tried to stand up; his complexion was grey, and he was unable to eat—but he saw. The cure turned out to be temporary; the eye doctor was called, and he struck again with his scalpels, hooks and scrapers. That evening he disappeared in his coach through the city gate. It was April 8, 1750.

Bach did not leave his bed again. He lived in total darkness and had a fever. Just before his death he had a pupil play him a chorale. The text contained a preview of being face to face with his Creator. Perhaps those present sang the chorale around the deathbed, in four parts, Anna Magdalena letting her voice ascend firmly against the underlying voices of the men.

Did Bach believe in this? He died "calmly and peacefully" according to tradition, at a quarter past eight in the evening. It was still light outside but the sun would soon set. Bach lived in the middle of the eighteenth century but with his feet anchored in the Middle Ages, thought the woman. Reason and empiricism were not inherent parts of his thinking, except when he was composing fugues. He believed; he trusted in the fact that he had a protector who was concerned about his lot. The second half of that century was easier, thought the woman. After the Enlightenment arrived, it was easier to project yourself into the way people thought. This death of Bach was virtually unimaginable, unless you saw him as a child who, in order to survive, yielded completely to his parents and experienced these parents as almighty guardians who would rescue him and always worry about him. How was it possible that the most intelligent composer of all time could have kept that childlike trust and transferred it to his religious thinking in adulthood? Because it had nothing to do with intelligence, of course. All over the world, at all times, among all peoples, people have created religions because the idea of facing everything alone is too painful; the knowledge that a person will disappear without a trace is too unbearable; the senselessness of human existence is too offensive. In a certain sense, yielding to the divine was easy because the fathomless boundless trust was preprogrammed as a survival strategy in the brain, in the developing thought structures, just like the capacity to learn language or to hear music. It was tempting. Who doesn't want to have a protector, who doesn't want to be SEEN?

The woman played the tragic variation and let the various voices sink in. The middle voice with its plaintive seconds.

Variation 25, Adagio

The bass that participated. The fragmented melody, stretched to the limit, that, fully aware, hurtled down at the end. The horrible dissonant in the last measure before the repeat of the second part: an F sharp and a G, very loud, at the same time, close together, struggling for a solution.

He must have known. That it was not true, an illusion. If you could give voice to despair and loneliness in such a way, you knew that there was no salvation and that, in the end, you were alone.

∞

Everything is different in the new house. It is so large—there are two staircases, and three toilets and a great many rooms. The familiar furniture looks smaller than in the old house. It looks lonely in the empty space. The way to school takes longer and runs past unfamiliar fields, through new shrubbery. Every morning the mother cycles or walks with the children and names the paths: where we saw the dead hare; where the parasol mushrooms grow; where the rainwater never runs off. When school gets out she is waiting on the square.

The father leaves for two months; he has to go on tour. When is he coming back? At St Nicholas, in early December. When it's almost dark when you get out of school. The number of nights is too many to count. The family shrinks closer together around the table. The babysitter comes more often than usual; the mother adjusts her work hours but usually can't take the children and pick them up herself. It's a raw autumn. The mother is too thin. She urges the children to put on their winter coats but she herself goes around in a cotton jacket. She coughs. She has a sore throat. She pays no attention to it. She catches a fever. She barely manages to call her neighbour and cancel work before she faints. The family doctor comes; he sees the frightened faces of the children and says: 'Your mother is very sick. We are going to make her better in the hospital.' The daughter nods and takes her brother's hand. She is already seven and can read, but he is still in kindergarten.

The ambulance drives right to the front door where no cars are allowed. When the mother has been placed inside, the ambulance cautiously turns the corner. The children stand in the door, the upset neighbour behind them.

'I'll read to you tonight,' says the girl. The boy is silent. His eyes are large with fear.

Improvisation, neighbours' help, the hegemony of the unexpected. The children sleep here one night, there the next. The weather remains turbulent. The boy refuses to put on other clothes and will wear stained, smelly warm-ups for weeks. In the hospital the doctors consider it is unwise to let the children come near the mother as long as the cause of the very high fever is not clear. Yet they go and visit almost every evening. They have to see that the mother is there.

In the morning the neighbour helps with the coats and the backpacks. She walks with them a little way, until the children are absorbed in a cluster of schoolchildren who all go in the same direction. At school they pretend that everything is normal, although they watch each other more closely than usual during recess in the schoolyard. The boy plays soccer with his friends; the girl draws chalk hopscotch squares on the pavement. In the classroom the lights are already turned on in the afternoon; the boy glues a steamboat in kindergarten class; the girl does her maths problems squinting her eyes, bending her left hand laboriously to avoid smearing the numbers. At the end of the school day all the children sit together in the big room. The head teacher reads aloud. It is so exciting that no one notices it is storming outside.

In the hallway the boy looks for his sister. She already has her coat on and is talking to the girl from their neighbourhood

Variation 25, Adagio

who is no longer their neighbour since the new house. Daddy is gone, Mummy is sick, I don't know yet where we'll sleep tonight—the boy can't hear it but he knows what she says. At the threshold they stop for a moment. The wind whips the trees and chases black clouds swiftly over the towering apartment buildings. The girl helps the boy to button his coat and then pulls the balaclava onto his head. They put on their backpacks and step outside.

∞

Finally the woman managed to get the right tempo, even a fraction slower than she thought, so that the movement came almost to a standstill and every note could be deliberately placed. She preceded the large reckless leaps in the melody every time by an appoggiatura, as if she was giving the melody a boost, except in the repeat of the second part, toward the end, at the very highest note. There she leaped without preparation, with a minimum of rubato, to the unornamented high D and from there, becoming increasingly loud into a thundering forte as she headed to the ending. If there is no protector, she thought, if I have to manage with the glum lover called Reason, then I'll scream bloody murder, then I'll shout against the wind at the top of my lungs.

∞

They walk over the path with the puddles. They lean forward against the wind. They stomp in the water with their rubber boots so that the water splashes around their ears. Then they continue walking. The girl takes the boy by the hand. He turns his head toward her.

'We,' he says, 'we.' She nods. Under the wild sky they go toward the empty house, hand in hand.

Variation 26

When they are fifteen or sixteen they want to go on holidays themselves. They still like to go with the parents, really, but they dream about trips with their friends: roaming through Europe; camping on a beach; white-water rafting in the Alps. Fortunately their imagination is greater than their organisational skills, and for years nothing comes of the plans. The mother knows it, keeps her mouth shut, and counts on deferral.

But there's no giving up. It's going to happen. It starts with a week on a Belgian campground, next to a stop on the coastal streetcar line. Then two weeks in the house of a classmate's parents, much too far away, with far too many children. The daughter recounts one disaster after the other: stolen passports; vomit on the terrace; fights about whose turn it is to cook, but that doesn't discourage her from new ventures. Her grasp of geography is rudimentary, and yet she seems to dance carefree across the world when she plans her trips. She is ecstatic when a winter sports holiday with college friends turns out to be in a small village where she used to camp with her parents. 'Then we can eat in the pizzeria with the checkered tablecloths. I know the place!'

Her underlying fear shows up in the form of travel nerves and miserable headaches. On the way to a train station or the airport the mother has more than once held the pale daughter in her arms, plastic bag at the ready. Yet she goes, the child, time after time, and overcomes setbacks and disappointments. At home the parents keep an eye on the telephone, promptly transfer large sums of money, and count the days.

She is twenty-two. She has studied hard and has worked; she deserves an extra holiday. Her girlfriend asks if she wants to come along to a hotel in the mountains; the hotelkeeper is a relative of the girlfriend; in the morning they have to make beds and in the evening draw beer, but in the afternoon they will be free. 'We're going by bus!'

The mother makes sandwiches. The father sees her off.

The first telephone reports are promising. The weather is beautiful; there is snow on the mountaintops, and the hotel guests provide amazement and amusement. 'They're so strict with their children, Mum, you wouldn't believe it! And they live for the bingo evening; then they start screaming, really.' The two friends give nicknames to the guests and start a photo project with the goal of taking a photo of every guest with one of the friends, without the guests' knowledge.

'Any nice guys?' asks the mother.

'I suppose so, I don't know yet. We're going for a hike now. With a guide. Bye, Mum!'

After a week, the tone changes. Is the work too heavy, the mother wonders, is she sleeping too little, is she drinking too much? Was the imagined situation nicer than reality? She is unable to find out. The daughter sounds depressed and evasive. 'I'll tell you when I'm back.'

"Tell" what? Something is wrong.

She looks pale when she comes home. After the first embrace the whole story comes out, with sobs and unrestrained gasping howls. A quarrel. A quarrel with her best friend. From the disjointed sentences and sighs, the mother is slowly able to create an image. Lack of sleep, bar service, beer. Among all the middle-aged guests with odd growths of beard and wrong socks, there was one nice young guy whom the daughter starts kissing in the courtyard near the crates with empty bottles, thus thwarting her girlfriend's plans.

The latter is indignant and disappointed: 'Yesterday afternoon I talked with him for an hour; I liked him! I told you, remember?'

Shame and discomfort for the daughter: 'I simply didn't think of it, one glass too many, it happened, just like that. It means nothing; I don't even want that guy!'

It couldn't be cleared up that night. Angry and sad, they fell asleep next to each other. During work they barely talked to each other. The daughter had a headache that did not wear off.

'The strange thing was that in the afternoons we acted as if everything was normal. We took very long hikes. We went mountain biking down a scary slope. We walked down a narrow path along a ravine. Together.'

Later the mother is shown photos: the daughter, with a fear of heights, who bravely forces herself over the mountain path, holding onto the rocks. The daughter in a cheerful pink jacket on a mountain bike, a forced smile. She balances on the ground with one toe and clenches her small hands around the handlebars so that the knuckles are lighter, even in the photo. Daughter and friend with sweet, dreamy faces, next to each other on a bench. Behind them the mountains tower majestically.

'It *has* to turn out all right,' says the daughter. 'Friendship is the most important thing. Without a friend life is meaningless.' Her chin trembles. 'She doesn't want to talk to me. Not about that. What should I do now? Shall I go and sit on her front step until she wants to see me? I have totally let her down—so stupid of me. She feels betrayed. She doesn't trust me anymore. Mum, help!'

Neither of the girls gives any more thought to the boy. He was only the test for the foundation of their friendship. He is superfluous.

'Write a letter,' suggests the mother. 'Then you can explain calmly what you are thinking and feeling. You can say how sorry you are. You can tell her what her friendship means to you.'

The daughter flings her remorse into the friend's mailbox. The mother sees with admiration how the child pushes aside her shame, how she dares to change and hold onto her new insight.

After a few weeks it's over. When the daughter comes for dinner she looks surprised at the holidays photos.

'I never dared to do that at all, walking along a precipice. I almost wet my pants out of fear. I wanted to be with her, do what she had planned. I'll never again go on a mountain bike.'

She hunches her narrow shoulders and shivers.

∞

Variation 26 was a hidden sarabande, a rather snappy melody in 3/4 time with a constant accent on the second beat of every measure, as is right in a sarabande. The melody was played now by the right hand and then again by the left, while the other hand produced a storm, a tidal wave of angry, short notes, in garlands and intervals, right through the dance tune. In the eruption of sounds, the melody was almost lost. The woman had to take care, she would have to be the guardian, the protector of the melody, but she let herself be distracted by the showy ornamentation. The garlands of notes went so fast that there was no time to play anything beautifully, no time to be aware of fingering or hand position—the only solution was to automate everything, to play through the spinal cord, not through the cortex, and when it was time, to plunge headlong into the sea of notes.

She practised small sections that she gradually knitted together, not too slowly. She decided which hand had to play where—above or below the other—and where the finger had to touch the key. The decisions depended on the correct tempo because in a slow tempo it made little difference since the muscles did everything; she had enough time to pull back a finger, lift a wrist. In fast-moving reality there often turned out to be only one solution. That is what she looked for and adhered to, so that her hands became trained in their correct, their only movement, and the wrists slid over each other easily, up, down, offering space to what the other hand had to say.

All the variations had two parts; both parts had to be repeated. Bach had composed it and written it down in that way; that was the convention in his time. Musicologists, as well as performers, assumed that in playing the repeat, changes were always made because the same thing twice was boring. It was customary to provide the repeat with ornamentations: trills, turns, grace notes. The woman did not like ornamentations. Ornamentations should be nice; you should enjoy them. But she did not. On the two-manual harpsichord for which Bach wrote this work you could bring about dynamic differences by pulling out the stop for another register. She could imitate this on the piano by playing loud or soft. Terraced dynamics! The same sound level for several measures, then increase or decrease step by step, a phrase at a time. That's how she had learned it at the conservatory, by imagining a wide entrance staircase for a stately country home. For a number of Variations she did something similar. Forte beginning, piano repeat, maintain piano in the second part, and close with the repeat in forte. Or everything the other way round, or two by two. If you thought about it carefully, there were four possibilities. On the piano there were of course many more options because you could make crescendos and decrescendos within one part; yes, Kirkpatrick didn't allow it, but it could be done, and she did it.

Glenn Gould sometimes left out repeats, the second one very often. At a dramatic conclusion this was certainly a way in which he avoided the problem of having to give shape to it once again. Sviatoslav Richter found this reprehensible. You had to play what the composer had written down. Richter listened to Gould's Goldberg Variations during a rare recital by Gould in Moscow, and later on a record. He was enormously impressed, thought it was brilliant, but couldn't get over Gould being so careless with the repeat marks.

'He doesn't play the repeats!' Richter said in a documentary about his life. 'You *have* to play the repeats. The music is far too complex to understand after hearing it just once!' He shook his head in despair. Such great affinity, such a great difference.

In this Variation there was no question of nicely embellished repeats. The music was so surprising that the woman couldn't do anything except let the sounds stream. She tried as best she could to emphasise the notes of the sarabande but sometimes had to let the melody disappear in the cascade of ornaments. The end of the second part was a passage that drove her crazy. Both hands moved up against each other, and the sarabande had disappeared and was swallowed up by a river of furiously rushing notes that flowed into a cascade that thundered down hard. No way to escape. Free fall.

Variation 27, canon at the ninth

This is the last canon, thought the woman. She walked cautiously to the grand piano, as if her body might break with an unexpected movement. She could barely hold her back straight and felt fatigue creep into her shoulders. It's the alternation, she thought, it's because I am making myself practise this endless cycle with its fickle emotions. Thirty-two measures of despair, thirty-two measures of rage, thirty-two measures of calm consideration. These abrupt changes drive people crazy, and if they are already crazy they become completely exhausted. I shouldn't go on about it; I should undergo it and then examine, disentangle, and overpower it. Not sigh. Think about the previous Variation and marvel at this new, clear structure.

Until now the two performing voices were always accompanied by a bass that supported, joined in, was involved. Here, for the first time, the two voices were by themselves. The contralto started. The soprano imitated her, in the distance, at a high pitch, at an interval of more than an octave. In the second part, after the double bar, the roles were reversed. The soprano set the tone, even in the inversion: ascending passages became descending, everything sounded different but at the same time, related. The contralto followed, imitated the soprano, and at the end, because the upper voice was already finished, was suddenly forced to be silent in the middle of a phrase.

The whole seemed simple as a two-part invention. Danger was lurking. The woman knew that she shouldn't play this piece "nicely," the intervals should above all not have anything spirited but instead seem rather lethargic. Let the finger come down and take it back calmly, a sixth higher and slightly softer one more time. That was the interval. Nor should it sound pedantic, and the tempo should not become too fast. She should balance on the edge of insensitivity. She would constantly have to be aware of both flanking variations with their burning haystacks, with their earsplitting sirens, their thunderclaps. In the middle of that violence this canon would be a bright haven. She would describe this state of affairs, simply and without bombast, almost naively.

Legato, the notes beautifully slurred? No, legato playing smelled of involvement, of feeling. Staccato was the opposite—you pulled things apart on purpose and demonstrated an almost ironic distance. It would have to be something in between, not really legato, not really detached, but part of the same context.

The last canon, the last chance.

Music taught you strange things about time, thought the woman when she sat for a moment with her hands in her lap, staring at the unornamented notes. Music transported you outside time, produced a state in you where there was not yet a question of time. Music filled you to such an extent that watches no longer ticked. Yet there was no medium that indicated the passing of time so exactly. Music synchronized the strokes of rowers, could make soldiers march in step effortlessly, let two thousand people in a concert hall breathe at the same moment. And music referred to her own silence because in every beginning an ending was announced. Despite the sorrow of the announced conclusion you longed for the unfolding of the melody, for the harmonies slipping by, even for the cursed ending. A puzzle.

∞

The mother leaves her car in a parking bay and walks hurriedly to the movie theatre. The weather is unsettled, along the sky rush grey clouds that sometimes even let through a streak of sunlight. There is humidity in the air. It is almost five o'clock.

Her heart leaps when she sees the daughter standing next to the revolving door. Still thirty metres to enjoy that sight, to look at the legs in the light brown boots, to smile at the deliberately unfashionable long coat, to admire the hair put up in a twist, the childlike jaw line, the neck, the hairs on the neck. She is there, thinks the mother, she is too early, she feels like doing this; it's a wonder and it's the most natural, the most familiar thing in the world. She is happy to see me. What does she see? A woman with a lined face. A woman who looks older, more tired, and thinner than she herself thinks. A woman who has been wearing the same coat for years because it's so comfortable. Maybe she only sees Mum; she sees someone who is happy with her. Their eyes meet.

It is pleasant to go to a movie at the end of the afternoon. The theatre is not even a quarter full. They sit down somewhere in the middle, place their purses under the chairs and slump back. The mother feels the daughter's arm against hers. On the enormous screen they see ads and previews. In the meantime they talk about the small, senseless details of everyday life. The daughter has cleaned her house, discovered a new shampoo, has actually almost finished her thesis. The mother smells the just-washed hair, would also like to clean the shed, the attic, but there are so many obligations on her calendar that it's better for her to sigh and stretch. The mother has annoying thoughts: why doesn't she let me read her thesis; why don't I tell her that I can no longer keep going, that I would like to quit my job? They rub shoulders when the movie starts, as if someone is going to tell a good story and they can listen together for one-and-a-half hours without having to do anything.

The movie, an enjoyable show about a boorish older man who in the end manages to adjust in a relationship with a big-hearted waitress, is entertaining, funny and well made. Mother and daughter are startled when someone is smacked, and laugh when the man, furious, curses at a minuscule dog. They remain seated during the credits, out of respect for all those people who have done their best. The theatre lights up slowly.

By now it is dark outside. In the restaurant around the corner they order lamb. A dark green herb has been chopped into the mashed potatoes.

"Fresh cilantro—you should make that some time. It's really good."

The mother sees the daughter eat and enjoys her obvious eagerness. No fear of getting fat, no distrust of her own impulses. After dinner they both light a cigarette. That is a bit less healthy, the mother knows it—she has set, and still sets, a bad example. They order coffee; the daughter eats all the cookies. Then paying the bill, putting on the coats. The goodbye.

'Next time a concert?' asks the mother. 'The Goldberg Variations in the recital hall, in a week or two. If you have time.'

'Call,' says the daughter. She is bent over her bicycle to unlock it. When she straightens herself, she turns her head with a sweep toward her mother.

'I'd like to, really! Just call to let me know when exactly, I mean.' She sees what I feel, thinks the mother when she watches her daughter's back and in the dark stands waving to nothing, to no one. I have to control myself; I can't take for granted that she wants to go everywhere with me. I have to leave her free. Not let her notice what it does to me. Why, actually? Shouldn't she know that I like to go out with her?

She shrugs her shoulders and looks in her coat pocket for the parking ticket. When she has found her car, she sits down inside and lays her head against the steering wheel. Next to each other, she thinks, just as we used to on the sofa. She was actually too old for it, maybe close to seventeen, but she snuggled up against me and let me put my arm around her. She wore soft terrycloth pajamas. We stared at the blank television screen. We just sat there a while, together. Maybe she dreaded the next school day; I dreaded her growing away, out of our house—I don't know. Each of us had our own heavy thoughts and leaned against the other without expressing them.

∞

Music disrupted and obscured the usual awareness of time, thought the woman. But you could handle that because through this same music you were placed in a clear framework. I search for deliverance from mercilessly flowing time, and the structure that saves me rubs finiteness in my face. I have to remain sitting on this piano stool until I keel over.

Not very long ago she wandered through a provincial city in Germany; it had been on the coast, probably Kiel. In the main street there was a music store with a decorated display window. On music stands there were pieces of cardboard with calligraphed statements by famous composers about the nature of music. She stopped and took note of it perfunctorily. When she turned around to walk away, she saw a piece of paper that had slipped to the bottom of the shop window. She bent down to read what was on it: "Music restores order from chaos, in particular, the relationship of man to time." She had pulled out her pocket calendar to copy down the words. Igor Stravinsky. The idea that she was restoring something with her stubborn and tenacious piano practising did not displease her. Yet the statement did not really feel comforting, but rather as if she were being called to account—by the conservatory director, by Stravinsky himself? His glasses had been pushed high on his forehead, above the long face with the downturned corners of his mouth. He looked at her with disdain. 'If you can't learn to have a better relationship with time, there is nothing more to discuss. Then you have no business being here.'

Punishment from Stravinsky, so what, thought the woman. I'll silence them all. Leave me alone; let me play this canon my way.

Variation 28

Contrary to her habit, she started with the scale in G major. In parallel motion, in contrary motion, in thirds, in sixths. Staccato against legato, forte, piano, crescendo, decrescendo. In octaves, with a thundering roar. Then an exercise by Brahms, a succession of seconds, pianissimo, with the smallest possible finger movements. The twenty-eighth Variation stood before her on the piano. Written-out trills. Below it, a leaping bass that followed the familiar pattern of chords. At every beat, the little finger of the hand that played the trill threw away a high note or a low note. It was difficult to keep the trills discreet in sound. She left them out and played only the bass and the thrown-out sixteenths, in the hope that they would start to form a sort of melody in her perception. As soon as she added back the trills, things became muddied. The tempo was wrong, it had to go faster, but then it sounded too hard, uncontrolled, and she hit wrong notes in the large intervals.

She felt incompetent, as if she had to make a new musical idiom her own, something that she was expected to have learned a long time ago, but that she did not master. She could listen to a CD, be able for once to hear how others interpreted this Variation. The fact that she made no move to do this meant that it was not supposed to happen. It was up to her what this music evoked, up to her alone.

And up to Bach himself, who was clearly working toward a climax in this virtuoso piece. The Goldberg Variations were almost completed. Only three were left. What remained to be said in that limited space? Too much, too much. The music came apart at the seams; the notes jostled each other on the staves, and the trills rang through everything. How would they sound on the harpsichord? As though you were clattering a tray of spoons and forks. A sound in which it was barely possible to distinguish a pitch. You would have to lift out the melody by rallentandos, agogic accents. That's how harpsichordists did it. Should it be done in that way on the piano, or could you do something with touch or pedal? If you made use of your pianistic possibilities, Kirkpatrick considered you a fraud.

What she did now had nothing to do with the performance of the piece. She practised; she did a kind of calisthenics for fingers and wrists and in this way deferred the real playing. Technique was never good enough; you could continue training endlessly without ever winning a match. Competition? Something had to be battled here; the music showed extreme tension. Something depended on it—that's how it sounded. It was about success and failure; it was a hard-fought victory, a triumph.

Before she could make all this into sound, a great deal still needed to happen. She would have to free herself from the chains of authentic baroque performance practice. In this variation Bach seemed to be pulling on the bars, he wanted out, to escape the limitations that the instrument imposed on him. What did "authentic" mean actually? Many present-day musicians seemed to think that an authentic performance was one played on the rickety set of instruments from the time when the composer lived. Anyone who doubted that, no longer counted. But didn't it show more respect if you linked the notion of authenticity to the intentions of the composer and not to the wood or the strings to which his period condemned him? Looking for the underlying intentions rose above the fumbling with violins rebuilt according to the original state, playing without vibrato, the keyless, perpetually out-of-tune flute, and did infinitely more justice to the musicality of the composer.

Except: what did Bach mean? Try and work that out. How they tuned a viola da gamba at that time, what registers were on a harpsichord, or how a grace note was performed; all of that was described somewhere and you could find it out. What you could not know is what Bach heard in his head when he wrote down these notes.

The woman suddenly had to think of her piano teacher at the conservatory. She had played an early Beethoven sonata for him in which there was a peculiar trio. Chords slipping by without a clear melody, clouds of sound that flowered just like that in the middle of a proper minuet.

'Odd, isn't it,' said the teacher. He came and stood behind her to look at the score. 'Do you know that the great composers, I mean the really great ones, sometimes reach forward to music that won't be written until a hundred years later? Here Beethoven writes in the idiom of Debussy. I sometimes wonder who among the present-day composers is anticipating the style of the next century.'

She had played the trio once again, with the left pedal pressed down and with liberal use of the right one. Now she thought back to her teacher's statement. She held him in high esteem; he was a real musician who could teach all of his students, regardless of their instrumental gifts, to play a beautiful cantilena. His ideas about the composer as fortune-teller surprised her. Did he believe that the future was fixed and that you could foretell it? In Haydn you already heard Beethoven, in Ravel, Stravinsky, but that was no big deal, in both these cases they were more or less contemporaries. What stood here on the piano was more remarkable: Bach as late Beethoven, as Brahms. There was time between those, and the question was, in which direction time had been bridged? The other way round, she thought. Bach had not looked into the future like a Cassandra when he composed this Variation, but wrote what he had to write. It had been Beethoven who looked back into the past. Just like Brahms, he had possessed a Goldberg edition. She imagined how Beethoven, on his almost modern grand piano had played the variations and, just as she was doing now, had lifted out elements that touched him. How he had later transformed and interwoven Bach's language into his own way of composing: reaching to the farthest ends of the keyboard, squeezing great forcefulness into the smallest form, the trills, the merciless trills. Then the thirty-two Variations in C minor were born, and later the Diabelli Variations. The same thing happened to Brahms. The finale of his Opus 21, number 1, the variations on his own theme in D major, had its roots here, in these ominous trills from which arose, with difficulty, a melody that was more or less hinted at rather than a finished one.

Bach. She experimented with the tempo. She was annoyed because her performance remained academic, limited, as if she was tapping out the rhythm with her foot. Let go, she thought, fly along on the fragmented melody, surrender. The measures shrank and joined together two by two, a heavy and a light one; her wrists danced across the keys, and the upper part of her body started to move along instinctively. It was a waltz! A desperate, deranged waltz. Here was dancing.

∞

High above the entrance to the hall hangs a balcony, where an old friend of the son and the daughter is busy with a variety of audio equipment. He has a bright green curly wig on his head. Deafening soul music blares from the loudspeakers. The hall is filled with young people, all between twenty-five and thirty, with shiny clothes and weird hairdos. They have glasses in their hands; they move slowly to the beat of the music, and they talk.

The mother understands nothing; because of the odd hairstyles she recognises practically no one and has difficulty locating her own children in the crowd. The son, a head of shiny silver hair, is doing the swing. The daughter, slightly wobbly on her high heels, comes toward her parents with outstretched arms. The mother sees the pale ovals on the inside of the tanned arms and only then looks up at the familiar face that is framed by a wig of thick black hair. The daughter's lips move. She pushes the parents out of the hall to the vestibule where the music rumbles slightly less loudly. There are chairs and sofas.

'For the old people,' she says. 'This way you can talk and enjoy things. Come here for a moment with your hair.' She puts sticky glitter on the mother's hair and fastens coloured clips in the strands.

'"Style your hair funky or cool 'cause both of us are done with school." That's the motto. I guess you don't want to, Dad?'

The father shakes his head and the daughter accepts his refusal without complaining.

'There must be at least a hundred people! Do you have beer? What do you think of my dress?'

Purple, low neckline, see-through. The openwork fabric of the skirt shows the girl's sweet, awkward legs. She holds up the pleats elegantly and takes a small bow. Then she dashes off to greet new guests.

The week before, both children finished their studies at the last moment—it's September. Different majors at different universities, the same thoroughness and cheerful narrative style in their Masters theses. It was a week full of movement between cafés, restaurants, auditoriums and cafeterias. While it rained outside, the son gave a lecture about his thesis in front of a filled lecture-hall. Two days earlier the sun shone while the daughter was examined. A real examination that lasted an hour, in a cubicle screened off by a glass partition that was supposed to pass for a room. The orange curtains that covered the glass partition did not close tightly, so that members of the waiting party could catch a glimpse of the examination if they had the nerve to walk up and place an eye against the slit.

'She's holding forth,' said the girlfriend. 'The water bottle is standing on the table, and she's moving her hands the way she always does. She's smiling.'

The father doesn't think it's proper to go and look. The mother leaves the circle of hopeful friends, who have flowers and beautifully wrapped presents lying next to their chairs, and walks to the examination cubicle. There she sits, the child, across from her serious instructors, in a white jumper and elegant boots under a nice skirt. Her face is slightly flushed, her eyes sparkle, and the nails that she deliberately stopped biting, are polished with a delicate shine. She looks younger than her twenty-six years, thinks the mother—or do you always take your children to be younger than they are? She leans against the cool glass and feels a strange mixture of pride and fear. How on earth is it possible that the daughter sits there with a straight back to defend the thesis that she devised and has written down herself? From where does she get the skill to face her questioners so frankly and disarmingly, turn her eyes from one face to the other, be quiet, talk, smile at the exact right moment? How can she drink water from the bottle that stands in front of her; how does she know that she is thirsty?

The mother feels a hand on her shoulder and lets the father lead her back to the circle of friends. Just a short wait, look at watches and at telephones, then the door of the cubicle opens. Triumphantly, the daughter strides out. Behind her stands the shy thesis advisor, smiling. He is visibly startled by the number of people and closes the door.

'Now they are going to give grades! It went well! I'm so nervous—I can't eat at all. No way.' She pushes away the hand of a friend who hands her a soggy sausage roll. She looks around the circle; she sees her friends, the parents and the friends of the parents and, sighing contentedly, sits down on a chair.

All of it went superbly, the daughter received high grades and a nice speech. With the empty water bottle in her hand, she gave an impassioned speech to her timid advisor. Afterwards everyone swarmed outside whooping, laden with flowers, toward the café.

The whole week was coloured by that elated mood. During the intimate dinner with friends of the children and of the parents, emotional words were spoken, and everyone felt good and contented. The daughter had snuggled on the mother's lap. With arms around each other they had looked into each other's eyes for a long time.

Accompanied by the music chosen by the boy with the green curls, the children's friends jump and dance in the hall in pairs, in groups, or alone. The son is leaning against the far wall and is talking with a fat cigar in his hand. The daughter drags him along to a table. The parents, from the vestibule, see how she makes attempts to climb onto it; weak with laughing she keeps falling back, it doesn't work, she sets down her glass and tries again, and finally lets herself be hoisted up by her brother.

Then both children tower above the crowd. The green-haired disk jockey stops the music; one of the boy's friends suddenly takes a guitar in his hands and sits on the edge of the table. He plays a few chords. A song from *Sesame Street* about the value and joy of school. The partygoers, who as toddlers watched that television programme daily, join lustily in the refrain. Then the boy and the girl look at each other and start a soul number in two parts, slow, serious, heartbreaking. Their voices wind around each other, improvising, one embellishes the other. They sway their arms above their heads; they have closed their eyes. They sing. Together.

The father wraps his arm around the mother's shoulders. From the warmth of his body she feels how proud and happy he is. This, she thinks incoherently, this, here, this joy—give yourself to it, lose yourself in it. She stares at her children; she squeezes her eyes into slits to sharpen the image but it only becomes more blurred; smoke coils through it, or she becomes blinded by the light flashes from the disco lamps, and the table seems a raft on a grey sea, a powerless couple of boards on which the children manage to keep standing, floating ever farther away from her view.

She presses closer against the father, she shares his pride, his joy, but underneath it grows into an inexplicable panic that feels like ice.

Variation 29

The day after graduation the whole world lies open, a range of almost unlimited possibilities, nothing has to be done, everything is possible. The girl enjoys herself. She spins around and every direction offers something new, something inviting. With her diploma in her pocket (in her pocket? Where is it? Lost? Already? No, in the wardrobe at the mother's house, for safety) she can go into any field. Retrain to be a pre-school teacher. Become a journalist. Still try voice training. Work at a publisher's. Television announcing. She doesn't know where to start. Girlfriends start at copy-writing agencies, get jobs at the municipal office, at high schools, in broadcasting. Her brother has suddenly become a diplomat and travels every day to the ministry in The Hague, dressed in a grey striped suit. The sister is proud and jealous. At this very moment when she can do anything, she has to reduce the possibilities and reshape the circle into a funnel, a trap that she will drop into and from where she cannot return. From where she can keep her eye on the others, the others who do more spectacular things that make her jealous. It's asking too much; it simply doesn't work.

'Go and substitute at a school for a while,' says the mother. 'You always wanted to become a teacher. Put off a decision if you're not sure.'

'Then I'll start liking it. Then I'll be stuck. I won't be able to let those kids down!'

The euphoria of the examination period pales. The house where the daughter lives is not miraculously cleaned up from one day to the next but remains the same damn mess if she herself doesn't take action. She has to fix her blown bike tire. To earn money she still works in the same restaurant. She has jumped across an enormous ditch and ended up on the other side in the same meadow.

The mother observes the rebellion and the sadness with unease. With a hint of guilt too. Couldn't she have prepared the daughter better for the effort required just to lead her life? The child has experienced enough difficulties during her student days, thinks the mother; it was a daily struggle to face up independently to that unsettled existence. She did it with effort, with almost too much energy. After every setback she resolved to learn something new. Salsa lessons after a miserable end to a love affair, a bridge course to overcome thesis problems. Behind her confrontation with treacherous reality, a child's fantasy has obviously remained: everything will be all right after the exam. That fantasy now collapses and the mother stands empty-handed.

She confers with the father. 'If only we could help her,' she says. 'If only we could choose a profession for her. And a husband.'

The father looks at it differently, calmer, more confidently. 'Let her go. She'll manage.'

And that's how it is. For the time being the daughter signs up with a temp agency and gets an office job that she experiences in her very own way. She observes office life closely and gives a hilarious account of it. Meanwhile she applies more or less secretly to publishing houses and television programmes and becomes alternately furious and dejected when this doesn't immediately lead to results. She takes a difficult journalism course. She visits a fitness centre three times a week. Now that she can't punch life into the desired shape, it's a pleasure to do it with her body. She becomes muscular. She has a racing bike.

She ends a passionate relationship plagued by problems in an adult and controlled manner. ('First take care of things in a responsible manner and go into therapy. We'll see again in a year.') The mother is surprised and impressed. In the sad aftermath, the daughter lets herself be won over by a man who appeared by chance and who terrifies her after a week. Naively trusting, she gave him her telephone numbers, and he knows where she lives. Sobbing, she calls the parents, has them pick her up, hides in her old room. A holiday to Italy with girlfriends comes as a liberation, as a conclusion, as a new beginning.

∞

Variation 29 followed the previous one seamlessly. The same tempo. With the trills and the frenzied waltz rhythm, Bach had started a momentum that now came to a climax. This did not happen in the music, as you might perhaps expect, by an increase of tones in ever shorter notes, but instead by a decrease. Longer notes, restrained movement, more sound.

The woman imagined how Bach had sat at his instrument; he had pulled out all the stops in order to produce as much sound as possible; he lifted his arms and dropped them one after the other in order to strike the alternating chords. He wanted to pound on the keyboard in these opening bars. He used so much force that the jacks with the quills that plucked the strings became detached. A string snapped. And another one. On a harpsichord you don't achieve much with force. Bach had to restrain his force in order not to ruin his instrument. The pent-up tension expressed itself as pain in the shoulder girdle.

'What in the world are you doing?" asked Anna Magdalena. 'It sounds so strange. Watch out that you don't demolish everything.'

He didn't answer, didn't even look up. He banged out full chords—crash bang, crash bang—measure after measure, and then with superfast triplets, played by swiftly alternating hands, raced down into the gravelly, rattling depth, where, playing the starting chords again, he came to a bouncing halt.

The second part started with lightning quick triplets that ended in rhythmically pounded chords and turned into a furious modulation to E minor, the "weak spot," the hole in the ice—not charming, not plaintive, but stern and determined. The triplets, now ascending by intervals of octaves, reaching up for the last time with so much speed, so much passion, that the conclusion came as a raging slash in the face of the listener. Anna Magdalena put her hands in front of her eyes and held her breath. He wanted to express something that was not possible—she understood that—but she didn't know what it was. What rage had to get out, which injustice was he ranting about, where did that immense despair come from? She brought her hands down and looked at her husband. How he sat there at the instrument that usually pleased him; how he clamped his strong jaws together; how he sat staring angrily at the two manuals lying above each other. She was ashamed for him and didn't know why. She opened her mouth, closed it again, and softly moved back into the hall.

Here Bach collided with the limitations of his instrument, thought the woman at the piano. Here he would really have liked a modern grand piano, a loud Steinway or a round-sounding Bechstein like this one. An instrument that gave you back what you put into it, an instrument that produced more sound the more heavily you touched it. A mechanism that could make the sound grow and explode, an apparatus that would be a worthy opponent for the muscle mass you used to attack it.

Tone was mass, tone was weight. You didn't need to pound the keys at all to be heard. If you hit the keys from a height, it created a chilly, dry sound. Loud, but ugly. The only thing you needed to do was: lower, drop, release. The weight of the released body part determined the strength of the tone—finger, wrist, whole arm, shoulders. The degree of relaxation determined the tone quality: full, warm. Power pianists sat waving their arms flamboyantly and were continually in theatrical motion; players of the controlled drop sat still and did no more than was strictly necessary.

The woman knew that from a physics point of view none of this made sense. A key went down no matter how you struck it; the hammer hit the strings, and that was it. Her sound theory was a physical illusion, but it was an audible pianistic truth. This penultimate Variation demanded the complete weight of the arms in the chords and the mass of fingers and hands in the triplet passages. At the end, she loaded the touch with more and more weight, until even her back and shoulders took part in the last triads.

The sound comes from the stomach and the legs, Sviatoslav Richter had once said in his melancholy voice. The woman liked the fact that he did not mention technique or musicality. He talked about the body. Playing the piano was biology, physiology, neurology. You had only a superficial idea of what happened in your brain when you were playing. You were imprinting, remembering, anticipating. You were feeling and creating. That you knew. Underneath cognitive and emotional activity, other, secret processes were taking place. You could express events, with their concrete course in time and space, in language, couch them in thoughts and feelings. The chemical translation escaped you, even though it took place in the centre of your brain.

Variation 29

The woman had immersed herself in the neurochemistry of trauma. What in life appeared as a disaster, marked in the brain a bombardment that permanently destroyed memory circuits, synapses and connections. A catastrophe dislocated a flood of cortisol that resulted in unparalleled destruction. You didn't feel it at all. Slightly shaky perhaps. Out of sorts. Not as if someone was carrying on with filleting knives in your head.

What could you do? How should you start to restore the dislodged connections? Was it possible to bring about any order in the chaos that had been created?

Playing. Playing the piano helped. Through laborious, extremely attentive, repetitive practising, the wounded pianist patiently worked to weave the connection between both sides of the brain. Every day, fibres were added deep inside the brain and the hippocampus, the hidden bridge that had been swept away, grew. Complete restoration was not attainable, perhaps not even desirable. The destructions caused by the trauma remained visible as silent witnesses. By playing the piano you built a footbridge, a wobbly platform that, at any rate, enabled you to walk around in the midst of the destructions and catch sight of the assaulted area.

Slowly and stubbornly, the woman practised the triplet passages. Without agitation and without expression, she drummed the chords into her head. Time passed and she did not notice.

∞

Summertime, the holiday season. The parents are in the north; the son is in the south. The daughter, returned from Italy, is in the city. She speaks on the telephone with the mother who sits with legs pulled up in a Swedish field, the phone close to her ear, her eyes closed to concentrate completely on the daughter's voice. The daughter flies alongside the water on her racing bike; she is on her way to her parents' house; she is tired;

she wants to get away from the city for a little while. There were guests in her house that she had to do all sorts of things with, Spanish guys who fortunately cleared out this morning. She cleaned up the rooms and now wants quiet. There is no wind, she says, it's warm and the evening is drawing near. She smells the water. Geese live on the banks of the canal, lying in the grass like white balls, but they don't attack her.

Without any prompting by the mother, she raises the subject of her future with surprising openness. She is going to substitute teach for a year; she already has the books, and yesterday she conferred with the teacher she will replace about the way to deal with difficult pupils. She has been accepted as a volunteer at the hospital TV station; she is going to make television programmes, learn things. She has resigned at the office and is breaking in her successor. Tomorrow, for the last time, the long bike ride to the office where she has felt so out of place. There will be a farewell in the cafeteria; she will get presents because they will miss her; they even offered her a permanent position. That helped, she says, it prompted her to take her life in her own hands. She sounds content. Soon, at home, she is going to open the garden doors, lie on the couch, turn on her favourite music. Sleep.

The next day the sun slowly creeps up against the sky of Europe and shines on an orange tent in France where the son is sleeping, on the wooden steps of a Swedish porch where the mother sits smoking after a nightmare and stares at the pale fog tendrils between the spruce trees, on a house in Amsterdam where the daughter gets out of bed to silence the alarm clock that she has purposely placed ten feet away.

What happens next has been reconstructed by the mother in the course of time, on the basis of a mass of data, among which are objects, photos, reports, and fragments of images.

Variation 29

The daughter throws her dirty clothes in a corner of the bathroom. She dresses in bike shorts and T-shirt; she takes a coveted summer dress from the mother's wardrobe and packs it in her backpack. She moves her racing bike outside and locks up the house. It is seven-thirty. She feels the sun on her bare arms. Water, pastures, suburbs, streets, an alley, the large square. A traffic light.

Amsterdam District Court, docket number 13-030801-01:... that he, without ascertaining whether the road was clear, manoeuvered his vehicle to make a right turn. To the question of whether he had turned on his indicator lights, the suspect answers that he doesn't know...

Public Prosecutor's Office, Court of Appeal, number 23-001974-03:...on being asked, the defendant is unable to indicate the size of the blind spot of his truck. He has never checked it...

Report of the coroner on duty:... massive, traumatic brain injury, resulting in death ...

Television news: the yellow trauma helicopter is suspended above the square, lands between the large church, the palace, the war monument. Policemen stand in a large circle; they hold up enormous white sheets to make prying impossible for curious onlookers. A twisted bicycle lies on the pavement.

The sun splatters the façades, it is still cool but it will be a warm day. The sun's rays warm the irregular, artistically placed stones that pave the square, brush the horror-stricken faces of the witnesses, caress the girl who lies there, her bare legs in the small straddle of death.

It is eight-thirty.

Variation 30, quodlibet

The woman, chained to her grand piano, contemplated the danger of travel. In a strange place you were separated from something to hold onto and control; away from home you had no idea what happened at the place you had left.

In 1720 Bach travelled to Karlsbad to give concerts for the prince who was taking the cure at the spa. A short holiday: walks through the park, drinking beer with colleagues, and every day the opportunity the play old and new compositions. He returned home rested, laden with presents, looking forward to a happy reunion with his family.

When the front door opened he felt fate glance off his face. Maria Barbara, his first wife, had fallen ill, had died and been buried while he was playing the harpsichord in the spa salon. The curtains were closed. It was quiet in the house. His wife's older sister, who was helping with the household, gave the shocked widower something to drink.

Bach wanted to have his children, their children, around him, and they came into the room one after the other: Dorothea, his eleven-year old daughter; nine-year-old Friedemann; and little Carl Philipp Emanuel, who had just turned six. They must have talked in subdued tones; perhaps they cried together, and most likely they prayed. Where is the little one, Bach must have thought, we celebrated his birthday right before I left; by now he's too old for an afternoon nap—why isn't he here, on my lap?

His sister-in-law shrugged her shoulders and went upstairs ahead of him. The dark grey skirts of her mourning clothes rustled. In the hallway a small boy sat leaning against a door.

'He doesn't believe it,' said the sister-in-law. 'He is waiting at her bedroom door until she reappears. He saw her carried out for the burial. Yet he won't believe it. He doesn't come downstairs to eat. He sleeps in front of the threshold. I haven't been able to think of a punishment; he takes no notice of anything. Friedemann takes him bread.'

Bach pushed her aside with an impatient gesture of his arm and went up to his son. The child looked at him with piercing eyes in his pale, pointed little face and then turned his head away. Bach remained standing and dropped his arms to his sides.

He grew up, small motherless, Bernhard. He learned to sing and to play the organ, and there was nothing wrong with his intelligence. Anyone who compared him to the first son from Bach's second marriage, born nine years later, saw a promising child next to a pitiable, feeble-minded one. The talented Bernhard needed no pity, he didn't ask for it, he asked for nothing. When he finished school, his father arranged for a job as organist in Mühlhausen, and when Bernhard ran away from there after a little over a year, Bach helped to find a position elsewhere for his son. The boy made debts that Bach discharged. He borrowed money that Bach paid off. He ran away again. He disappeared. Desperate, Bach asked the city council of Leipzig to start an investigation. Bernhard remained untraceable.

The report came from a completely unexpected corner: the University of Jena informed the highly esteemed Kapellmeister in Leipzig, that law student Johann Gottfried Bernhard Bach had died of a high fever just after his twenty-fourth birthday and, according to the regulations in force, had been buried in the potter's field.

Law? No organ playing? Studying instead of earning money? Bach started to get angry and anticipated more new creditors whom he would have to buy off, but fell back into his chair when the content of the letter sank in. There was nothing more to become angry about, there was nothing to pay off, and any care or help that he could offer was no longer of use. While summer began in Leipzig, Bernhard had died at a distance of several days' travel from his father.

Anna Magdalena was a conscientious stepmother, but she had her hands full with her own children. Her youngest son, Christel, was four years old and was already picking out tunes on the harpsichord. Bach used to take him on his lap and play for him. That no longer worked. The child didn't understand and angrily hit the keyboard with his little fists. Bach retreated to his study. Shaking his head, he fended off his wife's questions and denied the children access to his studio. During meals he sat silently at the table, and on Saturday evenings there was no longer any family singing.

Behind his desk Bach sat working on the aria that Anna Magdalena had once copied into her music notebook. With clenched fists he thought about the simple melody that Bernhard, too, had loved very much. When Anna Magdalena spoke to him once in a while about the dead child and tried to console him, he would silence her. He had to concentrate, he said, he was busy with a great work.

Variation 30, Quodlibet

That is how the unprecedented music that would later be called the "Goldberg Variations" was created; meant to animate the mood of music lovers, as it said on the first page. That was a lie; the most important purpose of the Variations was to preserve their creator from insanity.

For a year and a half Bach locked himself away with the music that became a vehicle for his despair. As the end came closer, he slowed the pace of his work. The structure that he had designed forced him to a conclusion that he did not want. He held his son close to him when he was absorbed in the Variations; he did not go mad with despair as long as he composed; he worked on a resounding gravestone for the lost child. Variation 30 approached; it had to be a polyphonic celebration, a triumphant conclusion of the series of nine canons that he had distributed throughout the work.

He tried to sleep. Dead tired, he stretched out next to his wife. She snuffed the candle, and darkness settled on him. He listened to her breath. He heard the children's beds creak on the top floor. When he dozed off for a moment, he fell helplessly deep into black earth; he saw a diagonal band of light become smaller and smaller; he could not scream, his throat was closed tight. Wide awake, with tensed muscles, he sat bolt upright. He braced himself in order not to get lost again in that horrifying depth. Lying down again, to surrender to the loss of control in sleep, was unthinkable. On getting up he noticed that his whole body was trembling. He snuck out of the room.

Where do ideas come from? From our dear Lord, Bach must have said, although he knew better. His inspiration for the last Variation, the "quodlibet," came from the treasury of folksongs that he had known all his life. The themes rang through his head, and he wrote down the fragments in such a rush that the ink splattered from his pen. Almost soundlessly he murmured the words 'I have been so long away from you, come here, come here…' and noticed that he moaned. The evenings. With children around the big table. Exercises in counterpoint by singing different songs at the same time, against each other. For four voices. The little ones led by the older ones. Bernhard with shining eyes, next to his brother Friedemann, two crystal-clear tenor voices situated between alto and bass.

Bach moulded the themes so that they fitted into the harmonic scheme; he counted the measures; he oversaw the whole. Although he felt a great urge to burst out in sobs, he didn't manage to press out even the smallest tear. With a clenched jaw he sat at the table and wrote.

The woman, who now had the written manuscript in a printed form in front of her, concentrated on the melody. It was a farewell song, she thought, and you heard that. It should not sound cheerful, not playful or fast or funny. The player was saying farewell to the Variations—it was almost time to close the score. Another, unutterable farewell sounded through the lines and the chords. She had to make room for that too. No triumph, but no sticking your head in the sand and pressing the soft pedal either. She wanted to move courageously through this quodlibet and do justice to every note. Nowhere in the whole work had she felt the nearness of the composer so much. It seemed to her that Bach took her by the hand and led her through this last Variation. She followed, without reservation.

∞

It is night. In the hall burns a dim light. The doors of the bedrooms stand open. From time to time the central heating boiler starts to roar. It is freezing. In the deserted living room the skates lie dripping on newspapers. The mother looks at them, closes the door and walks up the stairs. At the door of the children's room she listens to the small breaths of the boy and the girl. While she was reading to them earlier in the evening, their heads dropped heavily against her shoulders. She tucked both of them in and kissed them. Then she turned off the light and they sang songs in the dark. The boy fell asleep while the mother and the girl where still singing "Blowing in the Wind."

The four of them had been outside all day, on the large pond with its thick, black ice behind the house. The boy, beside himself with excitement, raced around on much too large racing skates he had borrowed from a boy in the neighbourhood. The girl, still insecure after last year's leg fracture, let her father pull her on a sled. She was wearing small figure skates with white boots. The mother pulled her up with both hands and together they carefully skated a lap. A neighbour came with a pot full of hot chocolate. The ice that was still smooth as a mirror in the morning was slowly being changed into a mysterious etching in grey and white by the skates of all the neighborhood children.

The mother sets the alarm and crawls into bed next to the already snoring father. Four bodies lie in the quiet house and she feels all of them fully. She hears the children although she knows that it's actually not possible. The boy mutters something in his sleep and turns over; the girls sucks in the air through her slightly opened mouth and exhales through the narrow nostrils. The mother sighs and slips into sleep.

Aria da capo

The pencil that the woman had used to write down her memories had dwindled to a pathetic little stump that could barely be sharpened. She looked up from the desk. Behind the wide windows the polder landscape lay stretched out in the sun. The water shone in the ditches between steaming embankments of dredged-up rubbish; sheep were grazing on the dike in the distance. Nearer the house two monstrous guinea fowl, escaped from a farm or a sanctuary, were scratching around. Once in a while they shrieked without visible provocation. Through the green idyll curved the narrow cycle path on which the daughter had ridden away. In the middle of those lush meadows the woman had seen her daughter's back for the last time. She was surprised at the intangibility of the landscape. The grass had not shrivelled; the ditch had not dried up. The destruction of the land took place solely in her head; outside, nature dressed itself in its most beautiful outfit: a lace collar of cow parsley along the path; a strand of bright yellow marsh marigolds in the water.

With masterful cruelty the landscape wiped out all misery and loss. The woman knew quite well that people experience the merciless continuity of nature as a consolation, but she felt little else but rejection and incomprehension.

The woman smoked. The cigarette was an ever-present lover who would in time most certainly betray her in a horrible way. He was going to abandon her, but for the time being he was at her side and nurtured her with deceptive faithfulness. In the corner of the room the piano was waiting for her. She had to call the tuner; the shine had again left the sound and an unpleasantness had crept into the tone that was the forerunner of being out-of-tune.

Her obsessive practising had made it possible for her to play the Variations better than ever before, better than when she was healthy and whole. That too surprised her it should be impossible for a damaged and amputated pianist to get that complicated work into her fingers. It had worked, despite and thanks to the injury. Imprinting the notes and disentangling the melodies had occupied her damaged brain. Every day she had been able to breathe freely for a time to the rhythm of the music. In devious ways Bach had given her access to her memory: every Variation evoked memories of the child, which she wrote down in the notebook. Suspiciously, because memories are lies. Restrained, because she wanted nothing to do with feelings.

She practised the Variations in groups to tune them to each other and to make them connect to each other. A constant, persisting heartbeat had to be heard throughout the work. Just as a human heart sometimes raced out of control and then again slowed down to a sleepy slowness, in the same way the tempo varied in the series of Variations, but always within the limits of physiological and musical plausibility. She strung the Variations together with an audacity that seemed like a mastery of the whole. Where did that conviction come from?

Mistrust suited her. She had written down imperfect bits of life and longed for these shards to join together naturally. She did not have much faith in her own memory; what was written down became a memory itself, and after a frighteningly short time, history and notes blended and it was no longer possible to determine what she actually remembered.

She had no choice. She did not want to write down the memories that lay in front, that she could call up at any moment to blazing life, although they had dominated her thoughts for several years. The woman grimaced, contorting her mouth into a sneering line, and tapped the table impatiently with the pencil stub. Reminiscences of that order could only be summed up in a dry list, without comment.

The endless trip home, in total shock. Trains, aeroplanes. The friends who stood silently in the airport arrival hall.

The cold child.

The house full of people, evening after evening. Those bringing meals, those addressing envelopes. Helpers.

The cold child.

The daughter's friends who kept watch for weeks on the large square, who stuck flowers and letters on the pole of the traffic light.

The house of the child. A piece of cheese in the refrigerator, a dress thrown on the bed, a half-written letter on the table.

The bizarre midnight trip to a parking lot in France to pick up the son.

The police, the doctors, the funeral director. The telephone conversations with authorities.

The cold child.

The sleeping pills. The inability to eat. The inability.

The washing, the dressing, the caring and tucking in. The small blanket, the doll.

The farewell.

Carrying the body to the burial. Seeing it off. Carrying. Setting up the place where she would be from now on.

Taking possession of the cemetery as an outside living room. Stamping your feet in rage at the closed gate after four o'clock.

Without any effort she would be able to expand this list to hundreds of subjects.

It amounted to the fact that everything had come to a standstill. But the treacherous heart continued beating. Just as every spring, the grass crept over the earth again, just as the buds on the trees masked the scars of the dropped leaves time after time, in this way something started to come alive here and there. Unwanted, indirectly.

Betrayal. The woman noticed that she could not bear it. She railed at new façades and re-routed tramlines. It took years before she understood that this was exactly the essence of life: change, replacement of one thing by the other. She did not wish to take part in that.

It was painful to see how intensely the girl was missed, although the woman thought that was appropriate. Young people, friends, bent under a sorrow that slowed them down for a considerable time and made them stand still. They could not and did not want to go on without her. Sorrow.

The woman was almost envious; what she felt consisted of a turbulent muddle of loss, confusion, and icy fury. It was impossible for her to get her feelings and thoughts under control. She turned to the piano for help.

She had distributed the child's possessions—blouses, books, cups—to loved ones. She used the girl's belongings in the kitchen and the bathroom. Sometimes she wore her coat.

All of it was doomed to disappear. The photos would gradually become mere images that only evoked their own memory. One day the jacket would be hung in a wardrobe, the soap dish would be lost, the bed linen would be torn. Already the daughter's scent no longer lingered in her clothes—the woman only imagined that. Later, when the parents would die as well—it had to be later because she was still there, every miserable morning—the movers would carry the remnants of the daughter's inventory out of the house and drive it to the rubbish dump.

It drove her into the arms of language.

For the woman, as for a very young child, music was a perfect vehicle to give form to her inner world. Just as a toddler, furious at the incomprehension of those around her, finally has to master words, in the same way the woman finally yielded to reality. She recognised that the lack of denotational force and narrative structure of music was a barrier to expressing her overpowering desire to describe the child. She was forced to have recourse to language. That was all there was to it. The pencil became an annoying friend who of course obediently wrote everything down that she dictated, but invariably it frustrated the fullness of her memories. It would have to suffice.

The words were a net to catch the daughter. Practically everything that seemed really important slipped through the mesh, and she was left with a sad, meagre residue. Whatever shone on the piano, settled on the desk as a lustreless, trivial statement. It made the woman disheartened. It didn't matter; it was easier to bear than the wordless misery that was at the bottom of all this effort.

She had torn herself away from the future. Never would she see the daughter pregnant, as mother, with the first grey hairs. The realm where the child was still visible lay behind her. She therefore turned around like the old Greeks, held time at her back, and devoted herself to translation. Floundering over the keyboard, she recalled fragments of the child's life, which she then converted reluctantly and tenaciously into language. She invented what was missing. During the whole process she was aware of the repetitive character. She repeated. The tragedy of the child's life was transformed day in, day out, into a gruesome farce in the hands of the mother.

The arm of the future gripped her neck, but that made no difference either. Life continued behind her back. That wasn't bad. She breathed at half strength. She didn't care. There was no other possibility. It had to happen the way it happened. The way she did it.

The score had shrunk. The Variations had become connected to each other, strengthened each other, contradicted each other, and made comments back and forth. Throughout the whole work a living heartbeat could be felt. The end came in sight. When the thirtieth Variation had faded away, she would have to play the aria, without repeats this time, as a look back at the very first beginning. A conclusion. A farewell.

Behind the windows the summer shimmers. Inside it is dark and cool. She switches on the piano lamp.

'Come,' she says to her daughter. 'I'm going to play something for you. I've worked very hard on it. Just listen.'

Then the aria blooms. The sounds of all thirty Variations vibrate along with each note, the simple melody pulls a train of memories effortlessly behind it. It develops with disarming obviousness. It contains everything that is dear to the woman.

The child stands next to her and looks by turns at the score and at the hands of her mother. The woman feels the warmth of the girl's body. She doesn't need to look, she knows exactly what the girl looks like. Just outside the circle of light from the piano lamp, the daughter's face hovers in the shadow, the teeth shine between the slightly opened lips, her breath sighs in the cadence of the music.

The future has retreated to the farthest corner of the room. Outside, life goes its unstoppable way. In a small world, free from space and time, the mother plays a song for her child. For the first time, for the last time. The girl leans against her shoulder.

'It's *our* song,' she says. The mother nods and starts the crescendo of the last measures; steadfastly she heads straight for the end. In the very last measure she will leave out the grace note and, without ornamentation, arrive at the empty double octave.

Within this emptiness is everything. Now she plays, now and always, the woman plays the aria for her daughter.